The Halfling's Court
A Bad-Ass Faerie Tale

Danielle Ackley-McPhail

with illustrations by Linda Saboe

PAPER PHOENIX PRESS

Stratford, NJ

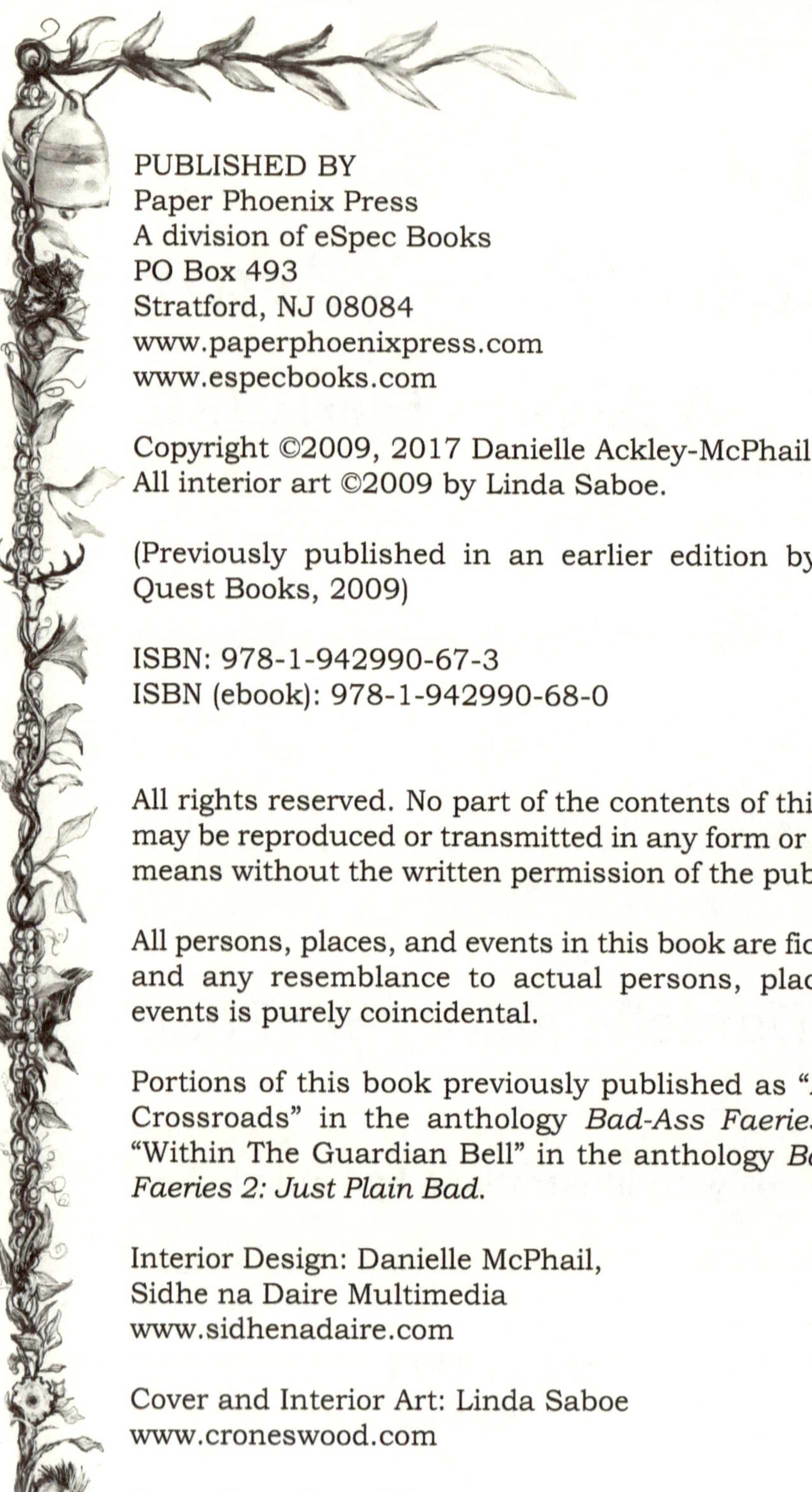

PUBLISHED BY
Paper Phoenix Press
A division of eSpec Books
PO Box 493
Stratford, NJ 08084
www.paperphoenixpress.com
www.especbooks.com

(Previously published in an earlier edition by Dark Quest Books, 2009)

ISBN: 978-1-942990-67-3
ISBN (ebook): 978-1-942990-68-0

All persons, places, and events in this book are fictitious and any resemblance to actual persons, places, or events is purely coincidental.

Portions of this book previously published as "At The Crossroads" in the anthology *Bad-Ass Faeries*, and "Within The Guardian Bell" in the anthology *Bad-Ass Faeries 2: Just Plain Bad*.

Interior Design: Danielle McPhail,
Sidhe na Daire Multimedia
www.sidhenadaire.com

Cover and Interior Art: Linda Saboe
www.croneswood.com

Copyeditor: Greg Schauer

Praise for Danielle Ackley-McPhail's Biker Faeries

"The latest from Ackley-McPhail features an intriguing mix of bikers and elves."
—Publisher's Weekly

"The Halfling Court is a well crafted and thought out book. The characters are immensely likable, and I found myself growing quite fond of them [...] a definite must read."
—5 Tombstones,
Bitten By Books Review

(From reviews of the anthology *Bad-Ass Faeries*.)

"Tugging at the readers heart and hitting all the right notes, "At The Crossroads" is just one example of the treasure trove waiting for readers in Bad-Ass Faeries."
—4 1/2 Mystique Moons, Sarah Gentili,
Mystique Books

"This was a very interesting take on faeries as you don't often hear of faeries being Harley riding, macho guys. I really liked that aspect of the story and the ending wasn't quite what you expected, but in a good way."
—5 Tombstones, Becky Gard,
Bitten by Books Review

"At The Crossroads" by Danielle Ackley-McPhail is one of the true gems in Bad-Ass Faeries. A fine, exciting tale with compelling characters."
—Jim R. Stratton,
Tangent Online

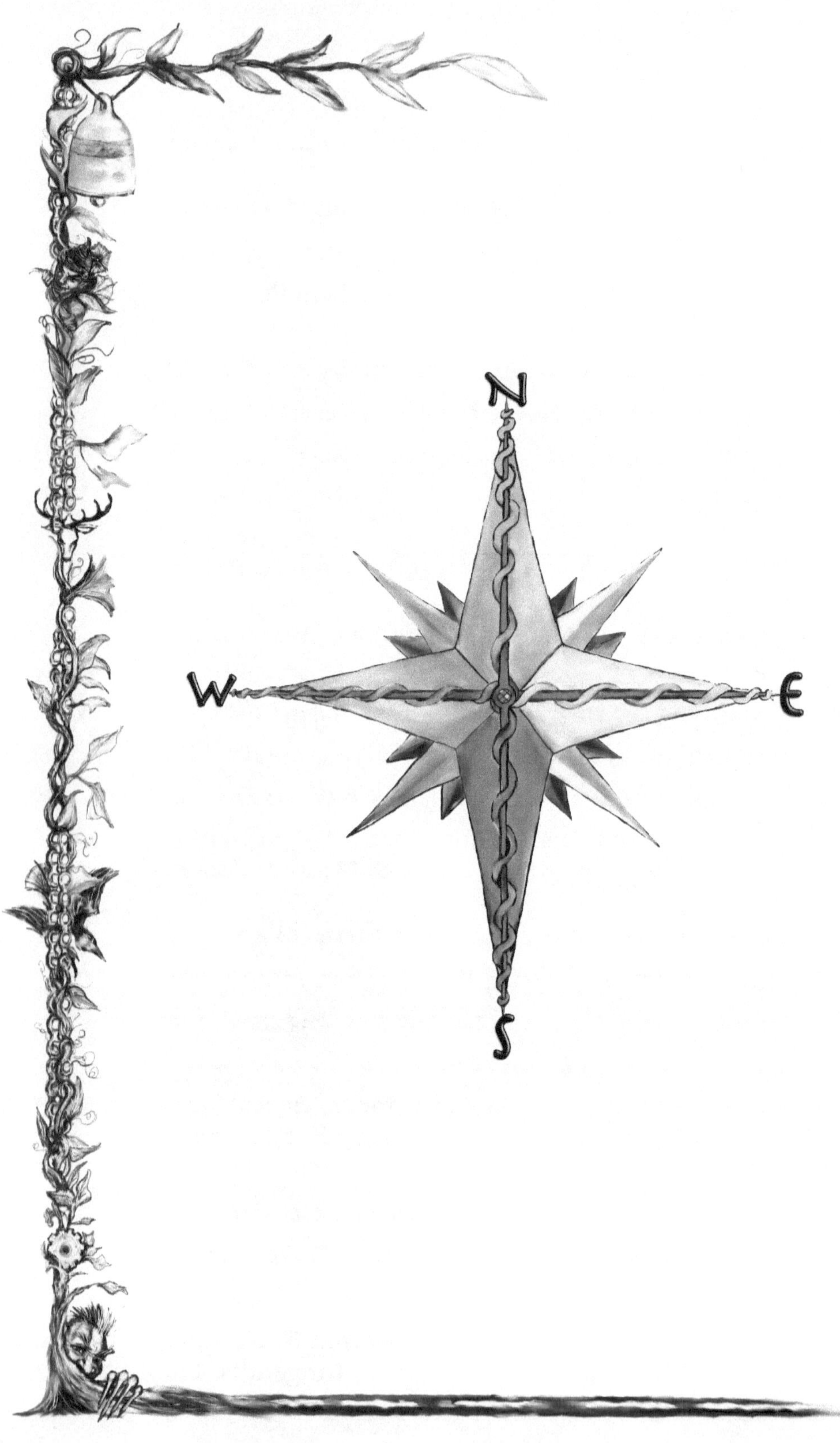

N
W
E
S

Dedication

To my parents, all of them:

Barbara Ackley and Sal Walter
and
Charles and Donna Ackley

Acknowledgements

I DON'T USUALLY DO THESE, JUST BECAUSE FRANKLY, I never really read them when they are in a book, but too many people worked too hard not to get a name in. First and foremost, I have to thank Linda Saboe for transforming my words literally into works of art and raising this simple book from interesting to spectacular. No amount of pay is sufficient for the time and effort that actually went into the illustrations in this book. I also have to thank the real Lance (my uncle), Jeff Lyman, Jennifer Ross, and everyone from the critical ms critique group for helping me to pound the text into something presentable, and above all, I have to thank my husband, Mike, for keeping me supplied in mint tea and macadamia nuts, and for giving up whole weeks of us time so that I could get this done by deadline.

Prelude

ANAIPHAL BATTLED FOR THEIR CHILD. IF SHE LOST HIM, SHE might live; if the child survived, she *would* die. Cameron felt ashamed of himself not knowing which to pray for.

Such was the way with curses.

He would never understand how a father, mortal or fae, could be so twisted as to wish ill on his own child. Anai's father, upon discovering she'd fled, had cursed her should she ever attempt to bear young that one day might challenge him. A death curse so powerful and vile it overcame the spell ring meant to protect her again harmful magic. Cam could barely conceive of such coldness. But then, what else would one expect from the guy sick enough to force his own daughter to marry him? And all in the name of power. Cameron still didn't know the whole story behind that situation, but he shouldn't wonder: the fae was mad. If not for her half-brother, Jonraphal, Anai would not have escaped her father's influence before her wedding night.

And now, because of Cameron, she faced death.

Cam's throat tightened and his gut went sour. Anai did not doubt she was doomed, but what of their son? Halfling births were not unheard of, but Anai could not say what impact the curse would have on the child.

Cameron sat behind her and cradled her gravid body with his own, desperate to ease her pain. He tried to quiet his fear, but gave the effort up as useless. The stink of it already hung heavy in the room. Cam shut down the forward-thinking aspect of his mind and focused all his attention on right now, this second, on Anai. His hands, both frantic and gentle, kneaded her arms. His lips feathered her brow with kisses.

"Help her." His voice ground out low and intent.

Jon's mate, Delilah, moved about the room grabbing the things they needed for the trip to the hospital. Jon had gone to get Cam's truck.

"Call them...'Lilah," Anai gasped. "Call them all, there is no time, and I shall need help in the bearing of this." Even as she spoke, a misty magic gilded her from the crown of her head to her clenched toes. Her abdomen rippled, wrenching a groan from her delicate throat. She seemed barely aware as Delilah hurried away to summon the fae members of their enclave. All of Anaiphal's focus remained fixed on their coming child.

"Augh!" Pain lanced through his wife until her body shook with it. Impossibly, a wild wind seemed to whip about them, as it swept across her, her grip on his hand tightened.

"Shhh...shhh...It's gonna be okay, baby. It's gonna be okay." Cam did his best to believe it, but the words felt empty, forced.

"NO! No! Cam...promise me....You must promise me he'll never know!" Her frantic plea sounded scattered and faint. "He must never know!" Then her fae kin filled the room and laid their hands upon her. Their eyes glazed and they stood rigid as they shared their strength, helping her bear the burden of the pain. Mouths parted in a collective moan and the room went taut with a sense of waiting.

As they diverted the drain on Anaiphal's vigor, the physical effects of her fear lessened; Cam felt her surrender to the labor. Her breath came in gasps until her words were but wisps; her body clenched and pulsed as fluid flowed from her womb. Cam watched Delilah move between Anai's thighs, pushing her legs up and to the side. The mortal woman placed her hand on his wife's abdomen just above the swell of her belly, ready to thrust, if need be, to force his son into the world. Powerless to help, Cameron clutched Anaiphal closer, his own voice murmuring a prayer.

Anai continued to mutter in between groans and screams of pain. As she bore down one final time, she dragged him closer. "Promise!" she demanded. "Promise he will never know!"

"Come on, Anai, focus!" Delilah said before Cam could answer, or even ask the important questions: who? and what?

Did Anai mean her father? Or their child? And what weren't they to know? Of the birth? Of his child's heritage? That Cam would be lost without his Anai? He growled in frustration. For a fleeting moment he hated everyone involved, with the possible exception of his wife. Then himself, most of all, for doing so.

"Promise!" Anai's voice trembled with panic.

Cam's gut clenched at the concern edging into Delilah's expression as she looked at him. He gazed back at his sister-in-law, not bothering to hide his confusion. She widened her eyes and mouthed the words, *just do it!*

"I promise, baby," he murmured close to Anai's ear, tears streaming unchecked into her hair. Anai continued to mutter and plea until everyone in the room promised likewise. The soft cotton of her shirt crushed in his grip as he felt a change take hold.

Their child came into the world accompanied by his wife's piercing scream. All the fae crumbled, just shy of spent...all but one. Anaiphal's face bore a fleeting smile at the solid sound of her son's bellowed displeasure. The smile faded away with the dispersing mist until the child's cry was echoed by his father's howl.

Lance

Chapter One

THE DUST ROSE IN A HAZE AGAINST THE TWILIGHT AS THE vintage '47 Harley-Davidson Knucklehead rumbled into the parking lot of Delilah's. Lance Cosain added his bike to the sea of chrome and steel overflowing the gravel lot into the surrounding fields and hemming in the barracks-style bunkhouse in the back. A kick of his heel set the stand and a twist of his wrist killed the engine. He ran his hands down his thighs, working kinks out of muscles tight from too many hours on the road, and turned a hooded gaze toward the roadhouse. He was home.

A thread of anticipation ran through his gut.

Lance swung himself out of the saddle. He removed his headgear and set it on the tail of the bike. Swirls of white paint hugged the back of the glossy black helmet. Celtic knotwork surrounded ancient symbols representing his name. He ran a finger along each bold line, feeling their power. As he traced them, energy crackled like static from the helmet to his hand. The runes flared, and then faded, leaving the gleaming surface an unbroken black. A gift from Suzanne, his faerie queen, the protective spell spread and settled over him like a second set of well-worn leathers, but stronger than Tri-Armor. It felt like she had just wrapped her arms around him and settled in to stay. He wished.

He headed for the entrance, his leathers faintly creaking and the power subdued. Pulling open the door, he stood a moment in the entranceway. Murmurs of "Wind Walker" traveled around the room as they recognized him. He acknowledged the nods and smiles as those filling the crowded space greeted him, their ride captain. Some of the bikers held up bottles, inviting him over; the mamas had a different invitation in their eyes. He made his way around the bar in search of Suzanne, acclimating himself to the ever-present smoke, savoring the comfortable musk, built up over decades, of butter-soft leather laced with the rich essence of whiskey and beer.

Lance searched the shadowy corners of the place for the slender platinum blonde with mischief bubbling in her silvery blue eyes. The room was large and open, with tables set up in the center and booths down both sides. He didn't find Suzanne at any of them, or at the bar that faced the door, stretching the full length of the mirrored wall. The lights were dim and the music loud. It was a simple place, no-frills, like its owner.

The one distinct feature of the bar: the Guardian Wall. Right beside the door, hundreds of brass cup hooks cover the wall. From each one hung a guardian bell. Some fancy, some plain; all of them free for the taking, or, preferably, the giving. Delilah kept the wall stocked because at *Delilah's* everyone knew road gremlins were more than just an urban legend. The bell represented a biker's protection, and the Hunt protected their own.

More than that, what made Delilah's special was the people....

Right now, it wasn't special enough: most of the faces were familiar, but none of them were his Suzanne. A slight chill of premonition ran through Lance, but he shrugged it off. She'd be here soon.

When the last rider arrived, they'd all get on their bikes and head for the meet-up, to join the Steel Horse Stampede for the sixty-five mile run down to Lynchburg, complete with police escort and a rescue-vehicle entourage. They'd ride in all their glory, with colors, hair, and spirits flying, alone or pillion, passing exit ramp after exit ramp full of idling cars as the stateys forced the cagers to wait until the procession went by, like royalty. And Lance, riding in the Front Door position, would lead the way, with his lieutenant and best friend, Gavin, riding the most trusted position of Sweep.

He could feel the wind flow over him already. He could feel the rumble of the road beneath his wheels and hear it echo endlessly at his back. And, God help him…again, he could feel the ghost of Suzanne's slender arms twined around him; hear echoes of her wild laughter by his ear, mingled with the roar of hundreds of cycles strung out behind.

"Sue," he growled in a tight, hungry whisper.

His eyes searched the crowd again, predatory and sharp.

"Hey, man, it's been a while."

Lance turned abruptly to see a tall, lean man with shoulder-length, golden-blond hair and bright green eyes that glowed with power deep within. Lance nodded, giving his best friend a comfortable grin. Gavin was Suzanne's brother. If he was here, she had to be around somewhere. Lance went back to scanning the place.

"She's not here," Gavin continued, as if reading his mind.

Lance's brow drew down low, and his grin took on a menacing feel. He turned away from Gavin and headed toward the bar.

"Suzanne's not here," Gavin repeated as he followed. "But she should be. She called two hours ago to say she caught some static outside of Dalton, and I was to let you know she's on her way."

She was coming! Delayed only by an encounter with the police. Lance closed his eyes and breathed, deep and slow. Then the rest of what Gavin had said broke through.

"Two hours ago? Dalton's not even an hour away. Was she havin' trouble with the Shovelhead?"

"The bike was runnin' fine."

Lance didn't know what to think. Suzanne was one of the best riders he knew; she should have been here by now. Why hadn't she called a second time? He wasn't comfortable with the possibilities that came to mind. "Anything else happen on her ride?"

Gavin considered the question. "She told me she had a run-in with a couple of BUGs a few days back, but she said it was nothing. A few insults. It looked like they might get tough, but a cherry-top cruised by and the guys backed off. She was fine; they were gone. I didn't think anything more of it…." His voice trailed off.

A slow burn devoured Lance's patience. "And you haven't gone after her yet?"

"I only just pulled in ten minutes before you." Gavin scowled. "She left the message at the bar."

Where the hell was she?

Lance slipped off his jacket and laid it across a stool. He had one certain way to tell if Suzanne was in trouble. Yanking up the shirtsleeve over his right arm, he bared a vibrant tattoo. To eyes not gifted with the Sight, the tat was of a gorgeous blonde provocatively posed, with her long hair feathered back and her lithesome curves draped in a brief, lavender teddy. To Lance the skin art moved and changed in subtle ways. It was Suzanne's most recent gift to him. A self-portrait. Whether she was by his side or miles away, the tattoo reflected a small glimmer of her thoughts and feelings. It was a link, a declaration. It gave him entry into her soul. It was how he knew, without doubt, that Suzanne loved him back. Even if things still stood in their way.

He angled his arm to get a better look at the tattoo. Suzanne's normally alluring expression was gone, her eyes were closed and her pale face slack, emotionless. Her limbs were posed as if bound behind her. A growl escaped Lance's throat before he could throttle it down. He locked gazes with Gavin. Gavin glanced from Lance to the tattoo and back again. A muscle in his jaw twitched.

"She's not dead. I would know...." Gavin assured him, though his eyes betrayed an uneasy tension as they lingered over the ink.

Lance's fists clenched. It looked like he was going to miss the Stampede after all. Grabbing his jacket, he spun around and headed for the door.

Behind him, someone tugged sharply on the segmented ponytail hanging halfway down his back. Gavin, of course. No one else would dare.

"Let. Go. Now." Lance bit off the words.

Gavin's hand quickly fell away.

"You're rushing off half-cocked," he said. "You know you don't have a chance of finding her without me. Just give me a minute while I make a call. Sue's got a couple of friends out that way; if she stopped by choice, that's where she'd head."

Lance didn't like it, but Gavin made sense. "Hurry up," he ordered, and moved to the bar to wait. Thoughts on his lady, he ran his hand over the intricate Wild Hunt MC design she had embroidered across the back of his jacket, a compass rose incorporating knotwork, the cardinal points, and the elements. Oddly fitting for their club, often scattered to the four winds, but still connected, though in truth it represented the charter members. The design...the tattoo...his helmet. Subtle means of linking herself to him, of watching over him. Of keeping him close....

Just not close enough, or she'd never have been taken!

Suzanne was essential to his life. His heart. He'd grown up with her and Gavin as playmates. They protected him from those who persecuted him for only being half fae, and he made them laugh, showing them the wonder of the world through mortal eyes. He could not recall a happy moment from his childhood of which they were not a part. They were as close as if they were born to the same mother. But Lance was thirty-five, or near enough; he wanted something more serious. And now, just as he and Suzanne were close to settling things between them, she'd gone missing.

His eyes locked on the front door. No more fooling around; time to find Suzanne, even if it meant riding the Knucklehead into the ground doing so.

"This is how you wait?"

Lance swung around to face Gavin. His lieutenant wore a hard, disapproving expression. Ignoring both the look and remark, Lance took a step toward Gavin. "Well?"

Gavin shook his head and Lance felt his temper flare.

"Clamp down, you're setting off Tilly."

Tilly...daughter of Jonraphal and Delilah. Lance's cousin through her father's side. They'd been raised together, as close as siblings. Thanks to a bastard who pulled an endo with Tilly riding pillion, she suffered from brain damage, reverted to a child-like state. She could handle simple things enough to help out in the bar, but throw her for a loop and she just couldn't cope.

Lance looked back and noticed her standing near the kitchen door looking agitated. Her lip quivered with a telltale tremble and the plate in her hand slanted until the food on it was in danger of sliding onto the floor. She was reacting to his emotional state. Not good. He had to deal with this, no matter how he itched to be on his way. He quickly tamped down his agitation, along with everything else he'd carelessly broadcast. In several strides he stood beside her. He took the plate from her hand and handed it to Kelly, who worked the bar.

"Sorry, Dumplin'." He slid his arms around Tilly in an apologetic hug. Careful to avoid the sensitive nubs tipping her shoulder blades, he gently rubbed her back, easing her distress. Power sizzled along the surface of his palms as he drew off the tension, defusing the emotion. He stopped only when she giggled.

Lance let out a deep breath. Like him, Tilly sensed and affected the emotions of those around her; only now, since the accident, she didn't have the control she used to have. Things went bad quickly when she got upset.

Very bad...

...For everyone.

Crisis averted, he brushed a kiss across her cheek and patted her arm. "Why don't you go see if they need anything in the kitchen?"

Tilly smiled and walked off, her chestnut hair falling in thick, wavy curls down her back. Lance watched her go, a gentle grin on his face. He loved his sweet cousin; he just wished the Organ Donor that made her the way she was now had survived so the club could have made him beg for death: he'd gotten off too easily. Again, Lance tamped his emotions down before they got out of hand.

A muscle in his jaw twitched and his gaze swept over the bar. The earlier relaxed atmosphere had disappeared. He'd dealt with Tilly, but he saw signs that his mood had crept into those around him. Time to split and find his lady before he owed his aunt for a new bar. Walking up to Gavin, Lance claimed his jacket, and they turned to leave.

A young kid intercepted them. His leathers were so new they still bore creases, and his colors were mostly clean. Lance would have pushed past him, but Gavin stopped beside the SQUID. The teen flushed a little as their gazes settled on him, but he stood steady despite the scrutiny of his ride captain and his lieutenant. Lance couldn't help but be impressed.

"What's up, man?"

"Was a couple of guys in here askin' about the Wind Walker earlier," he answered, his voice low but even.

Lance and Gavin exchanged hard looks. "When were they here?"

" 'Bout an hour ago, before 'Lilah came in. They weren't here long."

The kid's words hit Lance harder than the last time he ate asphalt. He felt scraped just as raw. Two hours ago Suzanne had called, then disappeared. Soon after, strangers show up asking questions about him. Hard to believe the two weren't related. But how? No human alone could overcome one of the fae, particularly a full-blood. Who among the fae had reason to gun for him? And was powerful—not to mention suicidal—enough to use Suzanne as bait? His hands fisted just thinking about it. His life without her in it would be very bleak indeed. Someone out there had decided to rob him of his joy, his love. Well, if they wanted a fight, they'd just ordered one express delivery.

He yanked on his jacket and pivoted abruptly, heading for the door. Gavin trailed behind him. They both stopped as they came face to face with Delilah. She gave a sharp nod. "You boys goin' somewhere?"

Lance growled. Everyone needed to stop getting in his way. He needed Gavin at his back. Blood called to blood. With Gavin along, finding Suzanne would be a simple matter of closing the distance and annihilating the responsible party. But Delilah had raised Lance; if she knew what was going down she would never let them leave alone. Lance didn't want anyone else along to slow them down or get in the way.

"Sue ran into a bit of trouble outside of Dalton," Lance said brusquely as he moved past his aunt. "Gavin and I are going to give her a hand."

"What about the rest of the club?" Delilah called out before he got halfway to the door. She closed the distance between them.

Impatiently, Lance stopped. "Run the Stampede. Gavin's with me, so Mongo takes Front Door, with you on Sweep. Keep everyone rolling. We'll catch up, if we can."

"You really think they'll make the run without you?"

"Delilah! You're wastin' my time! It's what they're all here for. Either they make the run, or they don't. Their call; it has nothing to do with me."

"You keep tellin' yourself that," she murmured, her gaze brutal in its wisdom. "These riders are here to make the run with you...with the Wind Walker."

He hissed through clenched teeth. "Anyone can be a wind walker; all it takes is treating people right, looking out for them on the road."

"Don't play dumb, darlin', you ain't blond enough to fake it." She gave him the eye. "You are *the* Wind Walker, and you know it. Everyone in here owes you some measure of blood. You can't take off and expect them to pretend you ain't ridin' off into trouble. These bikers are more loyal to you than they are to their own mothers."

Lance saw something more in her gaze than impatience, but now wasn't the time to figure out what. He didn't have time to argue either. "Fine...whatever. Just keep everyone here, for now. We'll call if we need the war wagon."

He turned away abruptly and walked out the door. His boots thudded hard against the walkway as he hurried to his bike. He already had a bowie knife sheathed in the top of his boot, but he wanted something more. He drew an expanding steel baton, or thunderbolt, out of one of his saddlebags and slipped it into the back pocket of his leathers. He then reached for his helmet. When he slid it on, the white lines of the runes and knotwork slowly swirled back across the glossy black surface as the power encasing him flowed automatically back into the gear. He took a few seconds to adjust to the change before mounting the cycle. From across the lot he heard Gavin's engine revving up.

"Hey," Delilah called out behind him. Lance glanced back and discovered that she and at least half the mother chapter stood clustered at the entrance. The rest peered out from beyond the bar's smoky windows. Every expression read fierce and loyal. "Keep the dirty side down, Wind Walker, and bring our Lady home."

After an hour of steady riding, Gavin throttled down, with Lance following suit. He looked around at the backside of nowhere, noting the untamed woods spread out along both sides of the road. The murky darkness beneath the canopy of overhanging limbs. The absolute silence throughout the wold...not even the underbrush rustled. A familiar sense of anticipation blanketed all.

Lance's lip curled as he spied the intersection ahead. Not much more than a dirt road, yet still enough to satisfy form. Apparently, his adversaries were into cliché. Well, this time they would regret this particular challenge. Lance swung off his bike and moved to stand next to Gavin, leaving his shield-spelled helmet on. He eyed the bowie knife sheathed along his friend's thigh. As if Gavin needed anything so mundane with *his* powers! Still, it never hurt to have a back-up.

Gavin had shed his jacket. Unhindered, his shoulder fins rose from where they lay, slowly unfurling like leaves in the springtime, up through slits in his shirt, expanding in reaction to the magical energy he drew about him in anticipation of battle. At the moment, the delicate-seeming limbs—already rising in graceful arcs bracketing Gavin's head—merely pulsed with muted colors, as if lit from within. While Lance watched and the power built, the excess trailed from the outer edge of the fin, fanning out into wings of pure, scintillating magic.

Lance grimaced and looked away, feeling a twinge of resentment. That was what his nubs should have been. And Tilly's. Only the human aspect of their nature interfered. Rather than manipulating energy with finesse, they broadcast emotion. More of a handicap than a gift, in Lance's experience. Making him more likely to set off a brawl when he needed to suppress one. Not that that happened much...he was always up for a good fight. Like now.

"Where is she?" Lance murmured, as he slammed his fist into his hand. His eyes strained as he tried to see deeper than the edge of the forest. "And where is the guy responsible so I can turn in his donor card?"

Gavin grinned and would have answered, but as he opened his mouth, the wind cracked down around them, shattering the unnatural calm. With a swirl of dust and leaves, it howled through the nearby branches. The perverted current snapped like a static charge through the two of them. Their hair whipped wildly, and their eyes squinted against airborne debris. Lance sneered again, unimpressed. Their unknown foe toyed with them. The bikers spread their stances in defiance, balancing against the wind.

"Where is she?" Lance's voice rose hard-edged. "Hand her over!"

The darkness swept out from beneath the tree line to engulf them as the raucous cries of a hundred ravens mocked his demand. The two bikers did not give ground. Feathered wings buffeted them and sharp beaks struck. They guarded their eyes, but did not waste their gathered energy on what was clearly a diversion.

"Enough with the games, coward," Lance called out, ignoring the trickle of blood running down his cheek. "Show yourself."

There sounded an explosive crack like a glacier splitting. The ravens scattered in a whirl of wafting feathers and strident shrieks. They took wing to the canopy where unease tinged their jeering caws.

Darkness gathered at the center of the crossroad, heavy and malevolent. Another crack, and the air rushed toward them in a pounding wave. Gavin's cycle crashed to the ground, causing the biker to growl. Lance fought to control his own anger. They were no good to Suzanne if they lost it. His breath came fast and shallow and his shoulder nubs smoldered, lending a faint, scorched scent to the air. Lance threw off his jacket before the leather—and Suzanne's handiwork—got damaged. His shirt was already ruined. His gaze flickered to Gavin with his fully formed fins trailing wings of multi-colored energy streams. Not for the first time, Lance cursed the weakness of his human side.

Suddenly, a touch like cool, crisp water ran across Lance's shoulder blades, soothing the intense burn. Gavin drew his hand away so quickly Lance almost missed the ethereal tug left in the wake of the calming touch. It lingered, though, an annoyance and distraction in itself. What was Gavin up to? Lance glanced sideways, out of the corner of his eye, but his lieutenant's expression revealed nothing.

Suspicious, Lance readied himself for attack. The malevolence seemed focused in the clearing before them…but what if that too was a distraction, like the birds? His half-human nature prevented him from calling on the magical energy present in all things around him, but it could not keep him from using his own, innate power. Gavin had taught him the basics. Lance drew upon that knowledge now, raising shields as strong as any created by the fae.

"Well done," Gavin sounded impressed.

The soft words were virtually lost beneath a sudden, unfamiliar scoff.

"How pitiful. You will hardly be a challenge to me, will you?"

Lance heard something that sounded off in the strange voice that came from nowhere, breaking the silence. It carried the cadence of fae speech, but resonated much harsher. Lance glared at the center of the crossroads as the growing darkness resolved itself into a tall, gaunt figure. Gavin cursed beside him. Lance empathized.

Before them stood a faerie clad in gleaming black leather molded like armor. His face bore no trace of softness, from an iron jaw to eyes like two chips of dark green granite. Black hair swept back from a high forehead to flutter around his shoulders with the sharpness of ravens' wings. Most disturbing of all were the fins rising above those shoulders, engorged with power, pulsing in deep, angry shades: the blue of death, the purple of a bruise, the green of decay…and the streamers flowing from them…iridescent black, like obsidian. They were ragged and pulsed in a way Lance had never seen before, so unlike the smooth, even flow of power of his fae kin.

Behind him, Gavin murmured, "The *Dubh Fae*."

"So, what's the deal with him?" Lance murmured back, but the dark faerie spoke before Gavin could answer.

"How fortunate for me I drew the first Hunt." The faerie's voice sounded harsh and flat, jarringly so. It lacked the rich depth normally characteristic of one of his kind. "The others will be quite disappointed to miss their chance at bringing you down, *halfling*."

Malice seeped from the *Dubh Fae* like poison from the back of a toad.

Lance sneered. "Didn't you wonder why your...friends sent you after me alone? I have issues with people kidnapping my lady. Return Suzanne now, and we'll only kick your ass. Make us take her back and God won't recognize you."

The faerie's hard, colorless lips curled in derision. "Your lady... I hardly think so. Still, let's make things a bit interesting before I do away with you, shall we?"

His adversary flexed his fins. His malformed wings snapped out, crackling and pulsing like something out of a bad B-flick. He looked like nothing so much as a ragged vulture, or perhaps a tattered crow. Any other time Lance would have laughed, but with Suzanne in danger, there was no laughing about anything.

Lance shoved all thought of the *Dubh Fae*'s appearance back when he saw what crept from the fringes of the forest. A handful of creatures separated themselves from the murk. They appeared as tiny, harmless old men. Their faces were wizen and each had a rust-brown hat upon his head. Their expressions epitomized malice.

They carried Suzanne between them, pale and unconscious. Her leathers were gone, except for her halter top. Her jeans were torn, and streaks of old blood matted her silver-blonde hair. Lance bared his teeth, his body tensed and coiled. The creatures clung to Suzanne's bound limbs, rubbing their faces against her in a way that seemed disturbingly endearing until he noticed the fresh streaks of bright red upon their caps and knew them for what they were.

Redcaps.

He had never seen so many at once. They were usually solitary fae.

They smiled at him in sly calculation, revealing vicious, shark-like teeth. They flexed their gnarled hands on her flesh and tiny tendrils of fresh blood flowed. One nasty creature dipped its head forward and flicked at the trail with its deep red tongue. Its expression was obscene.

As mad-eyed as a pooka, Lance unleashed his rage. He launched himself across the clearing, quite pleased that the *Dubh Fae* stood in his way so he'd get a chance to hurt him right off. Gavin followed close behind him.

"If you come a step closer," the *Dubh Fae* threatened, "she is dead."

Lance and Gavin stopped short only a few yards away from their nemesis.

The Black One sneered. He turned veiled eyes on the two who stood alone against him. His gaze settled on Lance, before flickering back to Suzanne and her guards. He then lowered his head toward the redcaps. "Service rendered calls for payment due." The creatures stepped away from Suzanne when the *Dubh Fae*'s hand flew out. Each finger glittered, capped in faceted ice. Gavin gasped. Lance spared him a glance.

"Dragon's Tears...." Suzanne's brother moaned. Corrosive to all but the hardest minerals, even the fae feared the substance.

"No!" Lance roared. But it played out too fast for him to stop. The *Dubh Fae* laughed again as silvery drops flew from the diamond sheathes tipping his fingers.

The world went dim and dark. The forest fell silent. And reality telescoped down to just Lance, the liquid death, and Suzanne.

It all took mere moments. She woke as the first drops struck her body. Her skin dissolved wherever they landed. The Tears sank deeper, quickly eating away her flesh. Blood flowed freely. And the redcaps collected their due. Suzanne bucked and screamed as they latched on until their caps were completely crimson and her blood trickled down their necks. She tried to summon her defenses but her magic flowed out along with her blood. Lance felt Suzanne's panic, her frantic grasping as instinct summoned back energy she'd invested elsewhere. Agony engulfed Lance as if something ripped his skin away. The helmet on his head shattered as Suzanne drew away the power fueling the protective spell anchored there.

Fighting past the jags of pain, Lance locked gazes with the *Dubh Fae*. From the corner of his eye he saw Gavin come up beside him. Lance waved him off, motioning him toward Suzanne. Confident his friend would do his bidding, Lance palmed the thunderbolt he'd slipped into his pocket and launched himself at the *Dubh Fae*. His opponent stood his ground, contempt in every sharp angle of his face. As Lance drew closer, the *Dubh Fae* brought his acid-tipped fingers around. Lance flicked his wrist to extend the baton and slammed the thunderbolt against the outer edge of the fae's hand, trying to turn the weapon on its wielder. He had the angle wrong. The Dragon's Tears fell impotent upon the ground.

The fae countered, blasted Lance with a ball of energy. He met the ground hard, but rolled to his feet. As he did, he drew his knife from its boot sheath and flung it at the enemy. It imbedded itself to the hilt in the fae's left wing fin.

The Black Fae screamed. His face mottled, and the struck fin slumped. The surface went grey at the point of impact and a gap opened in the energy tendrils forming the wing. The remaining span pulsed more erratically than before as threads of inhumanly bright blood trailed down from the wound. Pain creased the fae's dark features and a snarl twisted his lips. His rage rolled over Lance in waves that nearly inundated him.

His opponent's magic fluxed wildly, until he looked more mortal than fae. A glimmer of understanding began to kindle as Lance examined the fae more closely, even as he dodged another blow.

The *Dubh Fae* wrestled back control, whipping tendril after tendril of fae energy at Lance like a bullwhip. The attacks struck him, overwhelming his limited shields. Lance hit the road hard. His gaze fell on Gavin, who battled the *Dubh Fae*'s minions.

Gavin, his bowie knife in hand, fought off the redcaps still clustered around Suzanne. The fae scattered before the threat of steel. The crows, however, dove from the treetops in the hundreds, cawing and pecking with brutal precision. When they struck, their wicked beaks tore furrows in the would-be rescuer. Gavin wielded his blade with precision, but whenever a crow fell, another took its place. The cries of bird and man filled the air, as did shed feathers and shed blood. Neither side gained ground.

"Get her Underhill…*now!*" Lance bellowed as he rolled out of the way of another attack. Beneath the ruckus, a far-off rumble teased Lance's ear. He recognized the sound deep in his gut.

"You will die, Abomination! You and those that align themselves with you," the *Dubh Fae* said. His control slipped. The venom in his voice betrayed him. His magical attacks became both more forceful and unreliable. Rocks the size of Lance's head came zipping at him, only to fall to the ground at his feet. Angry flights of crows strafed him in formation. The ground heaved and the wind lashed out at him, some attacks connecting, others losing force before impact. Lance scrambled to his feet trying to anticipate the next strike.

Each second the Dubh Fae held them off, Suzanne faded further. She seemed to have neutralized the Dragon's Tears with her magic sufficiently that they no longer consumed her, but the blood loss would end her life if she weren't taken Underhill soon, where she could be tended and healed.

Lance pocketed the thunderbolt. Physically, they were at a stalemate. Instead he trusted his instincts and struck a different kind of blow.

"Abomination, huh? Recognize more than a little bit of yourself in me, don't you? Bet that bugs the hell out of you. Do the others know... *halfling?*"

The *Dubh Fae* snarled and stalked forward, an internal battle playing openly across his face. Each time the emotion flared, his magic faltered. Lance grinned wolfishly. At last, he understood his opponent: the *Dubh Fae's* magical side dominated, which is why he'd been able to hide his mixed blood among the Court, but the human half acted like a short in the circuit when his emotions ran high.

Lance leapt at the fae once more, hoping to strike a more physical blow while his enemy was distracted. But he did not act quickly enough. The Black One regained control and lashed out with another magical attack. Lance tried to evade, but again, his reflexes were too slow.

Crumbling to the ground with a groan, he felt his shields start to give out. The blood in his chest burned like liquid fire, as if it were suddenly as corrosive as the Dragon's Tears. Scrambling, he moved away and struggled to strengthen his defenses. Something blocked his efforts.

What the hell? He felt a tug, ethereal and fleeting, familiar.

The *Dubh Fae* towered over him. Disgust and loathing twisted his features. Lance braced for a final strike.

Beyond the *Dubh Fae*, Lance spied Gavin. His friend stood there staring back, poised as if torn between freeing Suzanne and coming to Lance's aid. Gavin's expression grew intent.

"I said get her out of here!" Lance barked at him.

Gavin ignored him.

Lance was going to wipe the ground with him for his defiance when this was all done. He watched Gavin's jaw clench as he raised his hand before him, his fingers splayed. He fisted them and drew back sharply.

The tugging Lance felt became a yank corresponding to Gavin's motions. Something inside him tore loose. As if their foundation had been undermined, Lance's remaining shields fell away just as the enemy's strike came down upon him. His heart seized in his chest, and his body arched...shook. He couldn't breathe. Through a haze of pain he watched the *Dubh Fae* laugh with satisfaction before whirling on Gavin.

Gavin merely stood there, his expression defiant, his arms still raised. Lance shook, anguish and outrage consuming his heart. Betrayal tasted bitter on his tongue. How? How could one who had been practically his brother turn against him? Had Gavin betrayed his own sister as well?

Lance's soul screamed as something died in him.

While he lay there in a daze, a rumble filled his head, the one he'd heard before, only louder. The sound of hundreds of engines roaring closer.

His vision dimmed. His eyes drifted closed. But the image of Suzanne, still in danger rose in his mind. He tried once more to call up some power, enough to raise his shields, or a final blast of emotion to heave at the enemy.

He couldn't do it.

Tremors ran thorough his body. The agony centered in his chest spread, rippled outward. And the rest of him...a force he could not see crumbled and crushed and pulped every inch. A force from within. His teeth clenched on a scream, convinced that something tore his bones out through his back. Meanwhile, he continued to burn as if dropped in a furnace, all his imperfections smelting away.

And it all took but a few handfuls of seconds.

His eyes snapped open, and the world became crisp and painfully clear. The air glittered and sounds he could not name flirted with his ears. Colors struck him as painfully vibrant. Overwhelmed, he squeezed his eyes shut again. He no longer felt like he was dying, though a part of him nearly had. Ironic that he had never felt more alive or full of strength.

A scream like that of a *bean sidhe* rang out, and wave after wave of fury crashed over the clearing. It swept over Lance with the comfort of familiarity. His affinity for emotions remained unchanged. He understood emotions. He spread his awareness to revel in the raw sensation. There he encountered an unexpected difference. Depth. He read so much more on the current. Knew who raged and why. Knew without a doubt, the wonderful, terrible things he could do if he reached out and claimed that energy. He allowed his eyes to drift open, already certain what he would see.

The Wild Hunt MC rode down all four arms of the crossroad, converging upon those in the clearing from every side. Delilah rode Front Door, with Tilly on the pillion pad. His cousin's hands clawed at her mother's shoulders, scoring the leather jacket. Tilly's eyes looked wild, and her lip twisted in a snarl. She epitomized the Furies and the Amazons of legend. She screamed her rage once more.

The crows fled. The *Dubh Fae* flinched as if struck, and the warriors from both sides froze in place. Lance climbed carefully to his feet. Tilly's rage called to his own. The love that fed it warmed him. Purposely, he loosed his control. Then he did something he'd never attempted before: he drew emotion from those around him, grasped it, shaped it, made it his own. The energy it gave him blazed at his back until the tattered remains of his shirt fell from his shoulders. He heard crackling in his ears.

Next he called to the supernatural energy spiking all around him. Never had he dreamed to harness it; he never believed he could, being only part fae. Apparently, he believed wrong. The magic came to his call. It flowed and wrapped around him. His shields rose again, unshakable. He grasped his new, two-fold power and took it in until it pressed tight against the inside of his skin. When he reached full, he took a deep breath and drew in even more.

And there it was, at his back, the wonder of fins unfurling for the first time. The crackle of excess energy shunting through those fins to form wings...*his* wings!

The *Dubh Fae*, confident that Lance had already been vanquished, made to strike out at the Hunt.

"No," Lance uttered softly.

The fae whirled, then hissed. Lance did not give him a chance to attack. Rage and fear and frustration, love and desperation and hatred, all balanced at his fingertips. He sent them crashing in waves over the Black Fae. The impact brought his opponent to his knees, his wings sizzling and snapping, then fading out as he fought off the emotions forced upon him. Lance recognized the shock and overload in the fae's gaze and had to wonder, had his nature just transposed as well? It looked so. *Dubh Fae* shrieked, and with his fae powers overwhelmed by his humanity, he opened another portal and fled.

The enemy vanquished, Lance turned on Gavin, pinned him with a cold glare. At some point Gavin's wings had faded and his fins no longer arched over his shoulders. He looked unrepentant. Lance saw himself reflected in the other's eyes: brilliant white wings arched high over his head. The rest of him looked much the same, though worse for wear, with his clothes in tatters. In contrast to Gavin, he looked imposing.

He strode forward to meet the fae. His hands curled into fists. Gavin stood his ground. He didn't tense, and he didn't back away. He just stood there, expectantly. Lance considered him for a long moment. Long enough for Gavin to shift where he stood, for a muscle in his jaw to twitch and his eyes to drop, betraying something of fear and something of guilt in their depths.

Suddenly, Lance understood what Gavin had done. The fae had robbed him of his shields long enough for the *Dubh Fae* to nearly "kill" his human half, bringing the fae aspect of his nature to the fore.

Grudgingly, Lance understood…but he still had issues with how it went down.

With his jaw clenched, Lance stepped around Gavin and hurried to Suzanne's side. Crouching beside her, he gathered his love in his arms, running his hands over her marred flesh. As he soothed her fears, he likewise used the fae force he still held to wipe away her wounds, envisioning her whole, something he had seen his uncle do in the past.

It worked.

Suzanne opened her eyes and looked up at him. She watched him in wonder, her own hand tracing his face, his fins, hovering along his wings. One sob escaped her as she burrowed against his chest. He pressed a kiss to her bowed head and held her.

"How...?" Gavin's stunned reaction to the sudden healing reminded Lance of their unfinished business. He waved Delilah over. She knelt beside him and took Suzanne in her arms.

Rising without a word, Lance turned back to Gavin. He slammed one fist into the fae's gut. The other connected with his jaw. Gavin took it without attempting to evade. He ended up on the ground, a wry smile twitching his lips as he rubbed his chin. Lance just turned his back and went back to Suzanne. With no sign of effort, he lifted her from Delilah's grasp and headed for his cycle with Suzanne cradled in his arms. Time to get her out of here.

As for the *Dubh Fae*, and the other unknowns who feared Lance enough to target him, let them come. Today would not be the only surprise he had for them.

"This isn't the end," Gavin murmured as he picked himself up, his words slightly garbled. "He'll be back, and he won't be alone."

Lance looked over his shoulder at Gavin, "You better worry about yourself, not what that BUG is or isn't going to do. You ever pull something like that again...you *ever* put the woman I love at risk again," he ground out through clenched teeth, "and I will kill you."

Gavin shot him a lopsided grin, "Hey, you even sound like one of us now...."

Lance scowled, thinking of the two halves still fighting for dominance inside him. "You haven't the first clue what I am now...and you better hope you never do."

He reached his bike and settled Suzanne on the front of his saddle. "Let's get you home, angel." Reaching down, he grabbed what was left of his jacket from the ground and wrapped it around her before turning back to Gavin.

"Let them come, we'll be waiting. Now mount up, I need you riding Sweep."

A glimmer. A gleam. A bright, intent gaze in the gloaming. Naught else betrayed the prudent denizens of the High Court. All lost interest in chatter and posturing; there was little point in it when their full attention was riveted on the dais.

Ker, or the *Dubh Fae* as he was more commonly known, made his way down the aisle and knelt at the foot of the Rowan Throne. The High King stood with a lethal grace, stooping like a hawk intent on prey, his beautiful, horrible face brought within inches of Ker's own.

"Such a clumsy effort, such a bald attempt to curry favor," the High King snapped. "You are not of this Court; you are here by my sufferance alone. Who gave you leave to act in our interest?" The words carried further on his whisper than they would have on a human's shout.

Ker flinched as the High King's fury rolled over him like heat from an inferno. Swept up in the massive eddy of the sovereign's displeasure threaded the lesser feelings of glee, disdain, and anxiety that swirled off the courtiers. Ker strangled the urge to lash out at the assault. The emotional barrage stripped him of any defense. By sheer will he staved off the impulse. He would not betray his secret shame to all the Court. Bad enough the hated halfling sussed it out. As for why he'd ventured the attempt at all, on that Ker also held his tongue. It would not do to admit that he had been egged into the ill-fated assault, not by friends, as the Abomination had presumed, but by enemies in the Court, who hated Ker for his differences, if not for his secret shame.

"Forgive me, *A Shoilse*," Ker murmured, the Gaelic for majesty rolling unbidden from him. It was the only sign of his unease that he would revert to that language of his long-ago youth, which he normally shunned. The courtiers shifted in anticipation as the High King snarled.

"Forgive you! You, who are unworthy? You force our hand, Crow! What have you accomplished but to draw this menace more swiftly to our door?"

The emotional assault battered Ker until it eclipsed his awareness of all others in the room. With a strangled moan, he forgot himself and looked up, his own rage kindling. He expected to see his death. Instead in the subtle shift of the High King's features he spied confusion and frustration, followed by a dawning realization that spoke more of Ker's doom, a much more unpleasant prospect indeed. An outside will pressed against his thoughts, faint and fleeting, followed by waves of outrage beyond the scope of anything yet expressed.

"Halfling!" the High King roared. "No wonder you failed! You are banished from *Sidhe na Daire* and this Court. Any that spy you in this realm are charged with dispatching you... permanently.

"We will deal with the halfling biker ourselves."

Ker barely heard the King's proclamation to the Court.

At that moment, he could not say which he hated more: the High King of Faerie, or Lance Cosain, the halfling leader of the Wild Hunt. Deep beneath his hatred crept a budding fear. Bad enough he stood a true outcast, stripped of any meager position he had garnered; how much worse when the High King learned of the new shift in the biker's power.

Smear

Chapter Two

SUZANNE WAS WORRIED. VERY WORRIED. LANCE HAD NEVER felt so much anxiety from a fae as what flowed through her now. The pillion pad behind him remained empty, but the unmistakable sensation clinging around his right arm concerned him. Sparing a fleeting glance from the road, he looked down to where the black muscle shirt left his arm bare. The tattoo image of his lady had shifted as only magic could allow. Right now the skin art hid itself between his arm and the curve of his chest, all four limbs wrapped tight around his biceps as if it were a lifeline. It was the closest he'd ever seen Suzanne get to being clingy.

Magic had seamlessly healed her body from the encounter with the *Dubh Fae*, but her spirit still bore those absent scars. Lance knew she was worrying about him. He even understood. Hell, he shared her worry. Not because someone had decided to target him, but because they'd hurt Suzanne, and she still wasn't over it.

Neither was he.

It had left him raw and sent him raging if he thought on it too long. This was the first time he'd left her side since he and the club rode to her rescue. He didn't like it any more than she had but it couldn't be helped…he rode on AMA business that couldn't be put off. He'd been on the road a week.

Suzanne wasn't handling the separation well.

Again: neither was he.

The second they cut him free he'd jumped on his bike and headed home. Didn't gear up, didn't check the weather. Didn't even take the extra time to call and let them know he was on his way. That's how his fool ass ended up riding unprotected in conditions even a SQUID would have had more sense than to ride in. Of course, the weather had been nice when he'd headed out. Not so much now. His teeth ground against one another and he resisted the urge to rev his engine.

Suzanne waited safe at *Delilah's,* surrounded by the other members of the club. He had to keep telling himself that. Though mindspeaking was not one of his gifts, Lance thought real hard at her. *I'm coming, babe. I'm coming.*

The power of his engine thrummed through him, making him one with leather and chrome and steel. If he listened real close, he almost dared believe he heard the mad tinkling of the tiny pewter guardian bell Suzanne had attached to his swing arm before he'd left. No way was the bell actually audible over the sounds of the engine, but he certainly sensed its magic, subtly flavored by Suzanne's special touch.

Behind him, the hiss of four wheels on wet pavement blended with the muted rumble of some cager's engine, a reminder Lance needed to keep his mind on the slab. As if to reinforce his thoughts, a Q-Tip in an equally ancient Buick passed too close on Lance's left, sending the bike swerving toward a rainbow-covered puddle.

"Ah, crap!" Lance swore as his tires hit the slick and lost their grip on the road. The Knucklehead dipped sideways, surely setting the bell to ring wildly. His stomach lurched hard until he brought the bike vertical once more.

"Get some glasses or give up the license, Grandma!" Lance yelled after the oblivious old woman.

He fought the skid and won, but it was close. If he'd wiped out in this weather he'd have surely earned himself another set of broken wings.

That settles it, he thought, *time to get off the road a while.*

A quick glance down at his gas gauge confirmed it was time for a fluid exchange, anyway. Lance moved into the Bike Lane and opened the throttle, triggering a string of horn blasts from the cagers to either side as he passed them by.

As the biker rode away down the center of the road, the puddle bubbled and seethed. Up from its shallow depth popped an odd, tiny creature, clutching at its ears. "Smear doesn't like the faerie-man. Not at all. Or his bloody little shrill bell. Smear wants to grind his face, crush the bell." Crouched upon the road, he slammed his thick, meaty fists against the asphalt.

Microfissures formed: the conception of a pothole.

Another of his kind crawled up through the fissures, and then another, expanding the damage to the roadbed until the puddle drained away. A troupe of inch-high gremlins stood where it had been. They appeared identical in every way: Skin as grey as asphalt, with an oily, rainbow shimmer. Hair long and thick and spiny, like a porcupine mated with a box of nails. A thick white line marked the center of their faces like war paint, and along their arms ran thick, black squiggles. Like tats or tribal markings, only with the dull gleam of tar snakes. Each finger looked like a spike, reminiscent of those found at toll booths, only jointed. The miniscule troupe rumbled and grumbled as they watched the bike speed away.

"Smear doesn't like him, wants to snap his bones, crumble a fender," one of them muttered. "Smear doesn't like him, wants to bash his head, crack the tranny," added another. Each of them offered up the world of pain they planned to inflict upon the biker and his cycle; each of them punctuated their threat by pounding upon the blacktop, splitting it further.

Why do you wait? He escapes you! a lethal voice hissed into each of their heads. As it did, their eyes flared bright green instead of red. The voice sounded beautiful and horrible all at once, leaving them as cold as icebound pavement.

"Why? Why? Smear doesn't wait! We go! King-fae says we can; says we must. Smear listens," they vowed in one voice. "But King should know, biker's been belled."

Go, now! I will take care of the bell, the king's voice answered.

Cackling a sound like shattering windshield, one gremlin grabbed the next, each of them melding until there stood only one the size of a particularly ugly cabbage patch doll. It crouched upon the roadway as a Mustang went zooming by. With supernatural precision Smear reached out, his spiky digits piercing the vulcanized rubber as if it were water. Swinging up, he perched on the rim of the wheel, his fingers still in place. It wouldn't do to have the ride spin out...until after Smear reached his target, anyway.

As they sped away, the only sign the gremlins had been there was a scattering of nail-like spines and the crumbling edges of a pothole just waiting for the next car to come along.

The rain had settled down to a pissy mist by the time Lance pulled into the truck stop and right up to the pumps. Kicking down the stand, he unscrewed the gas cap, setting it on the saddle as he got off the bike. In minutes, he'd topped off both his gas tank and the reserve and headed inside. With the rain letting up, he didn't want to stop long, just enough to fill up and drain.

"What'll you have?" asked the hot, young mattress cover in a waitress uniform. Lance kept his expression neutral as she gave him the once-over, making it clear she offered a bit of distraction along with whatever he wanted from the menu. She was good. He practically felt her gaze run from his segmented ponytail clear down to his ass. Too bad he also felt the ribbon of malice spiraling through her, focused on him. One of the dubious benefits of being an empath....

He'd never even seen her before, so what was her hang-up? He might have suspected she was a part of the *Dubh Fae's* crowd, gunning for the halfling, only he couldn't sense anything fae about her and that crowd loathed humans nearly as much as they did halflings.

"I'm good," he answered. "Just looking for the way to the john..." She acted disappointed on the surface, but Lance sensed her satisfaction, as she pointed down the hall.

By the time he came back the waitress was nowhere in sight. Lance frowned and glanced around the diner before hurrying outside. Nearing his ride, he discovered where she went. He stalked up behind her and cleared his throat.

"Oh!" She spun around. Her hand slid into her apron pocket while her eyes shifted to the side as if looking for where to run. Instead she laughed, slipped on that fake invitation smile, and let her eyes roam over him suggestively once more. "I just had to come out for a closer look. Nice ride..."

"My old lady likes to think so," Lance let a bit of steel creep into his voice. "Now, how about stepping away from the bike..."

Again, that flash of malice deep in her eyes.

Before she could say a word, a couple of drivers came strolling out of the truck stop. "Hey, Jolene, Mac's lookin' for ya," one of them called out. With a huff, Jolene hurried away, her eyes slicing across Lance in a much different manner than moments before.

"Whack job," he murmured as he inspected his scoot. Everything seemed in order. He couldn't find anything that she might have disturbed in the short time she was alone with the bike. Even the bell still hung in place. Dismissing the episode from his thoughts as just one more example of everyday craziness, Lance pulled out his cell phone and hit the speed dial.

"Hey, bro," he said as Gavin answered. "Just checking in. Nah, I'm about half an hour out.... No, everything's fine. Tell Suzanne I'll be there soon."

He flipped the phone closed and slipped it into his pocket, then he swung onto the bike and gunned it out of there.

Not far past the truck stop, Smear released his grip on the wheel where he'd hitched, letting the spikes shred the treads as they pulled away from the rubber. As he flipped himself to the ground, there was a *pop,* and the tire blew, followed by the crunch of crumpled metal. Not as glorious as Smear would have liked; just a bit of bent steel and a bumped head, no blood or flame or final breath. Several Smears broke away from the whole and, despite all reason and their one-inch size, they shoved the 'Stang and its unconscious driver out of sight of the road where the biker would not see it before scampering back to meld once more.

"Faerie-man, crunch your head, hose your ride," the gremlin chanted. "Dance in your blood and wear your stupid bell as a hat."

Continuing to mutter, Smear stalked to the center of the road and called every bit of Smear from every crack and crevice, every slick spot and crumpled zone. As they rallied forth like blowflies to roadkill, the gremlin beefed up, absorbing all that came until he was the size of a pitbull, and then a Rottweiler. He stood there in fine fae challenge, idly whirling a bit of chain swept up from the side of the road.

The roar of the cycle drew near. Smear crouched at the ready, blending with the asphalt like a chameleon on a log. Only a chameleon never had such teeth.

Lance throttled down. His head came up, and his muscles went taut. If he used Jolene's malice as a baseline, what he sensed now shot off the charts. Pure malevolence pounded at him from every direction except above. He strained his senses trying to pinpoint the threat, but his perception seemed off now that his fae nature dominated the human, rather than the other way around.

(He still didn't know if he should thank Gavin for that, or redesign his anatomy. Of course, the encounter at the crossroads would have gone quite differently, possibly even fatally, other-wise.)

Anyway, if Lance believed what he sensed right now, surrounding him were a crowd of people who hated him...only they were all invisible.

Not totally impossible...he should know...but frankly the only ones that hated him that bad were all fae, and he didn't sense them.

Lance kept going, but took it slow, just in case this wasn't his empathy acting screwy. Drawing a deep breath, he gathered in magic slow and easy. His body shook in reaction as the energy filled him up. He grinned at the still-new sensation of his shoulder fins unfurling. Every nerve ending seemed to dance in reaction to the magic trailing from those fins as they rose through the slits in his muscle shirt to form his wings.

Man, I almost *sympathize with those 1%ers addicted to meth. If it feels anything like this, no wonder the craving's damn hard to shake.*

Ready to blast whatever came at him, Lance rounded the bend. He could see no source of threat. The road remained smooth and bare. Writing it off as his body adjusting to the recent changes, he opened up the throttle. This close to home he had no interest in taking it slow.

Out of nowhere, the wind rose, sounding like ground glass and a cackle mixed in a blender. The Knucklehead hit a bump camouflaged by the roadway. Again the front wheel threatened to skid. Lance growled and fought it, only to hit one on the other side.

All around him the wind both whispered and howled.

Goin' down, faerie-man, crunch your head, shred your wings.

Goin' down, faerie-man, spill your guts, blow your gasket.

Goin' down, faerie-man, skin nothin' but rash, bike nothin' but trash.

Goin' down...goin' down...goin' down....

"What the hell?!" Lance swore. There was nothing around but him, the wind, and the road.... So what was the deal with the voices in his head? Mindhearing wasn't one of his gifts any more than mindspeaking was. His lip twisted in a snarl and his brow dipped low, as he opened up the throttle all the way, ready to power through this creeped-out stretch of road.

What was that Irish blessing?

Oh...yeah.... *May the road rise up to meet your feet....* Someone needed to tell them that wasn't necessarily a good thing.

Before his eyes, the road rucked up in front of him. Malice met his gaze from bright red eyes glowing like lit brake lights. A chain whirled idly in the creature's hand. Any moment Lance expected the links to fling out, tangling in his rims. Maybe that was why he wasn't quite ready when the chain dropped to the asphalt, and what could only be a road gremlin incarnate launched itself straight for him.

Yeah, there was that hatred loud and clear now. It still streamed from all around, but that made sense; Lance was surrounded by nothing but road...and gremlin.

"Bring it on, skidmark." Lance sneered. He had faith in the bell Suzanne had gifted him, knew its magic firsthand; it served the sole purpose of either warding off gremlins or trapping those already in residence on any bike. And as it was a gift from a loved one, its power was doubly potent.

Between the bell's protection and his own magic Lance felt little threat from the gremlin.

Goin' down, faerie-man....

"...Yeah, right!"

Even as Lance watched, the Knucklehead collided with the creature. The gremlin shattered into countless pieces. Only they didn't fall away. Each one grimaced with hatred, trying to stare him down with light-bright eyes.

They cackled and again he heard the grind of shattered glass on the wind. That was when Lance realized something was wrong with the bell. The swiftest of glances confirmed it still hung from his sidearm, but the clapper remained silent and he could no longer sense its magic. Then he remembered Jolene, crouched by his bike, and he cursed with enough venom to put a goblin to shame.

Goin' down, faerie-man...crack your balls like a walnut, crumple your pipes real good...chew you up into itty bitty bits.

One of the buggers chomped on his earlobe, making him regret he hadn't yet replaced his shattered helmet; another slammed a fist full of spikes through his engine block. The others followed suit, in one manner or another attacking him or the Knucklehead. Lance snarled and fought to keep the bike stable while smacking the creatures away. But there were too many of them. He could hear the bike start to fail; smell fluids he ought not to have been able to smell...both his own and the bike's.

Tearing one of the creatures from his neck, Lance roared and slammed the bike into a skid, laying her down on the road, scraping dozens of the gremlins off as he surfed the asphalt. Both his wings and the cycle sent up sparks. Little puffs of acrid smoke peppered the air where the gremlin bits ignited. He felt some satisfaction in that, but there were too many of them left for it to count. He leapt to his feet, leaving behind a good bit of both leather and skin, but snatching up his bell on impulse and pocketing it.

His left arm felt rawer than ground chuck, and his pants were almost as torn up. The road rash would hurt like a bitch later, but right now it just stung.

Goin' down, faerie-man, goin' down right now, put you out like a candle.

"Come on and try it, slick," Lance growled. "See how fast I jack you up."

The gremlins hissed at him as they gang-banged back into one creature. Its bulbous nose twitched and its finger spikes flexed. It stalked forward, now roughly the size of a bull mastiff, only much uglier.

Lance's wings crackled behind him as he lashed out with a side kick at his adversary. The kick sent the creature flying, slamming it right into the downed bike. Lance winced at the added damage; the gremlin, on the other hand, merely exploded back into a thousand smaller selves. They scrambled to meld back together as Lance stalked forward and brought the heavy tread of his biker boot down on a choice few of them, leaving nothing but smears on the pavement. But too many remained. He quickly faced a once-more unified foe.

Bloody bells! Bloody biker! Smear smash 'em and crash 'em and leave 'em in pieces!

The gremlin fairly frothed as it spat and cursed. It also gave itself away. Lance knew what to do. He again dropped the creature with a kick. This time, the gremlin anticipated the strike and mostly kept itself together. However, while it was distracted reabsorbing the few bits that popped loose, Lance drew out the bell.

With a vicious grin, he held it up high, dangling a silent threat. But was it an empty one? Lance could see the clapper was gone, hastily ripped out by the bitch at the truck stop.

Still…nothing that couldn't be overcome… He might not have been able to manipulate magic until recently, but that didn't mean he had no understanding of how it worked. Drawing a bit of magic to his fingertip, he drew it down the slope of the bell. There sounded a subtle hum that turned Lance's grin wolfish. In his thoughts, he pictured a clapper of pure, hard light. The more he focused, the more solid it became. For a fraction of a second, the creature missed a step.

No! Turn you to pizza, tear you to shreds, crush the fucking bell like a bug!

The gremlin's raging took on a frantic edge as it launched itself at Lance's hand, spikes extended as if to slice the bell. With a laugh that any member of the club would have known to back away from, Lance sent the bell ringing right in the gremlin's face.

Once in flight, the gremlin had no hope of avoiding the hollow. Caught fast by the mage-energy clapper, every bit of the creature disappeared within the depths of the tiny bell. It rang even more, frantically swinging as the gremlin fought his new prison.

Nothing escaped the bell but sound.

Lance smiled and gave the bell a little shake of his own…noting that it rang with a new tone, like screeching metal against metal. The sound delighted his ears. With a satisfied grin he slipped the bell into his pocket and righted his battered bike. That's when he noticed a Mustang buried in the brush on the side of the road. Propping the Knucklehead beside it, he pulled out his cell phone, hitting speed dial as he flipped it open.

"Yeah, Delilah…. I need you to send out the Wrench…."

The king was not amused.

He could not see the stretch of slick pavement where his minion took on his rival. Dair sat on his throne and listened to the disjointed muttering of the gremlin, which told him precious little of the conflict. He concentrated harder, trying to hear beyond the elemental's babble, but to no good end. The effort woke a pounding in Dair's head, which fed the rage that simmered constantly in his veins. His fingers rasped the surface of his living throne until he felt its protest deep within the grain. The sensation drew him back, loosened the grip of his temper just enough to send him to his feet. He paced the edge of the dais; the faint light caught a glimmer of white gold on his right hand. Another subtle reminder. He clenched his fist and swept the empty Court with eyes the color of oak leaves in deep summer. He found himself alone in this merging of glade and hall with nothing but the acid-drenched muttering of the gremlin and his own chattering suspicions as company. The fae of the Court had fled to their bowers; wisely, Dair had to admit.

A shudder took him, followed by another. The empty hall seemed an omen foretelling his decline in power, mocking him as king of a barren Court, where once the fae had thrived beneath his rule, when the lovely Tisaphal sat beside him as queen. Now the living boles of the tree-grown walls likewise taunted him. They were chronicle trees—an organic record of fae history going back countless millennia. Pivotal moments in each reign imprinted on the flesh of the barkless trees in the written script of the fae. The length of the Hall stretched as far as he could see with the glorious eras of High Kings past. Then his queen lay murdered, and soon after his children betrayed him, placing their own desires above the welfare of their race. His rule had been as glorious as any other until that faithless day, the last openly recorded on the wall, now hidden. The effort did no good; all knew the events recorded. His shame forever etched in the ageless wood and immortal memory: thrice betrayed by members of his own household and his own blood decades ago. From that day forward the foundation of his reign crumbled. He'd allowed no other moment to be revealed; though none could break the documenting spell, his druidic advisor, Gort, had found the solution: he'd forced a shielding of heavy bark upon the chronicle trees, entrapping future etchings deep beneath, hidden from all and unable to expose further weakness. Dair wheeled back to face the supposed seat of his power, his gaze both hungry and hating.

The throne stood on the raised dais, polished and carved, its bole and boughs shaped to contour his frame as he sat upon it, only the upper limbs of the *Rudhu-an* tree remained in their natural state, the bark smooth and silvery, crowned by high leaf fronds sporting, in disregard of season, both clusters of small, deep red pomes and corymbs of white flowers. Another reminder of how tight he must hold on to his rule. He was oak, not rowan, and thus he had never quite sat easy upon this throne.

In defiance of the betraying thought, Dair climbed the dais and sat once more, closing his eyes as he breathed deeply, his will bent toward a far-away stretch of highway where a mere gremlin strove to deal with the newest threat to Dair's power. The gremlin's yammering was indistinguishable, his agitation high. Some of that fed through the link Dair had established when he'd charged the creature with this task. Tension arched the High King's back and his fingers clutched again at smooth, polished wood. The click as his teeth snapped tight echoed loudly in the empty hall. The ghostly scent of charged ether spoke of magic performed far away, filtering through the gremlin's senses. Foreboding rose in Dair like floodwaters.

He'd been told the halfling had no magic.

Doubt and suspicion surged. Who plotted? Who lied? Who else thought to challenge? His fae features twisted, grew ugly, as fury and paranoia flourished. Dair began to lose his connection and fought for calm until the link no longer strained. He shuddered and came to his feet at the ringing of a bell and felt the distant magic surge. It had the clear, crisp essence of fae magic, *familiar* magic, but it had a bite like sharp iron, which Dair felt at the back of his tongue.

Impossible!

And yet, he felt the frantic tug of the elemental's panic, followed by agony and such tightness he could not breathe. A cold chill settled over him and his vision darkened. Dair fought the sensations off. Drew back just enough to be free of them, yet still connected. His chest surged with each new breath and something dark simmered at his heart as he heard a mortal laugh, no longer obscured by the gremlin's ranting.

An icy smile played across Dair's lips as he listened to the halfling's call. Plans took form as the High King saw the potential opened up by his henchman's failure. Rather than sever the link with the gremlin, he strengthened it, worked it, changed it until he was safe from feedback effects, while still being aware of all his connection could tell him from the other side. An unexpected edge salvaged from failure. Now, to harry the opposition....

He extended a mental summons to his champion. Forming plans, Dair left the Court for his private chambers. The dark elf already waited at the door when Dair arrived.

"*A Shoilse*, you have need of me?" Callan was one of the few that had been a member of the Court before the time of betrayal.

He was loyal beyond measure. At one time he'd even entered into a betrothal agreement with Dair's youngest, the faithless wench.

"Our hand has been forced, my warrior," Dair answered as he swept past into the grand bower, a curious mix of room and glen, lush greenery and decadent comfort intermingled in an organic symmetry. He lowered himself upon a couch of thick, green velvet moss while Callan remained standing upon a natural marble floor. "Unsanctioned war has been engaged with the rabble that call themselves the Wild Hunt, mortals and halflings and outcasts of our own kind. You will command our forces and teach these bikers what their insolence has earned them. Then draw them near until we crush them between us."

Callan swept a formal bow, his long, lean frame lowered, one knee bent, the other leg extended as his right hand brushing head and heart and earth, then straightened. "I go to serve," he murmured, and backed from the room, head inclined. His eyes seemed to hold a glimmer of malice.

And then Dair found himself alone once more, keeping company with his doubts and suspicions, pondering what he could not help but suspect. He murmured and cursed. His clawing fingers tore swaths from the moss beneath him. Random bursts of magic scorched fist-sized patches into every surface until Dair's manner scattered the will-o-the-wisps from the oak branches that made up the ceiling and sent them fleeing to other chambers in an effort to escape his brooding ire.

Dair na Scath found himself in darkness both without and within.

Suzanne

Chapter Three

Lance climbed out of the truck cab and slammed the door behind him. Davey, the Wild Hunt's Wrench, didn't say a word. He was already at the back, by the trailer, preparing to offload what was left of Lance's prize Knucklehead.

"Leave it," Lance ordered, leaking a bit of the menace he'd carefully reined in on the drive. "It's goin' to Cam's." This was not a happy thought, and more of Lance's control slipped.

Davey tensed and froze, his expression darkening. Lance took a couple of deep breaths and tried to get his emotions locked down, but the bell in his pocket shook violently, reminding him of the encounter with Smear until his temper surged. Pushed to the edge by the emotional leakage, Davey's gaze hardened and he launched himself at his captain, the only target around.

Cursing, Lance sidestepped the other man's fist, which slammed into the door panel, caving in the metal. His impulse was to throw himself into the fight, to tear the Wrench apart just to release some steam. Between the bell and meddling fae—the *Dubh Fae*, the High Court, the gremlin...even Gavin—Lance's control had eroded, while his power cranked into overdrive. Not good, and man, did it piss him off.... No fucking way his emotions were going to get the best of him like this.

Davey rounded on him again, ready to rip his face off. Lance side-stepped him and locked his arms around the biker from behind. His left arm screamed as Davey bucked and swore, pulling skin away from scab, but the Wrench couldn't get free. Lance took deep, steadying breaths, and focused on letting go of his anger and frustration. Then, with a finesse he hadn't had mere weeks ago, Lance drew off the other man's fury. Once he'd harmlessly dispersed the emotions he released his grip on Davey. The young man staggered a step away and shook his head, as if to clear it. His chest heaving, he spun and stared at his truck. Horror and confusion rippled across his face as he turned incredulous eyes toward Lance. On a groan, he squeezed them shut, pain in every tense line; they stayed closed until his breath slowed.

"I'm sorry, man. It's not your fault," Lance said. "I'm raw, and kind of messed up, since...." The words did nothing so he let them trail away. He took a step back, his hands falling to his side. "Go ahead, you deserve a shot."

The Wrench's eyes opened slowly, then, staring up from under his brow, he shook his head. His tension stood out clear, and Lance understood. The rider had attacked his captain. Members had been cut loose—or worse—for less. But Lance knew Davey couldn't be blamed; he'd only channeled Lance's own emotions. He couldn't hold that against the guy.

Davey turned away, back toward his truck. His fingers gently ran across the dent, the tips trembling. The hand shook as he palmed it through his hair. The damage wasn't bad, but it had to hurt; that truck meant near as much to Davey as Lance's bike did to him. He empathized, even without his gift.

For him, the Knucklehead represented more than just a sweet ride or a powerful piece of machinery. It represented hours upon hours upon hours of painstaking work as Lance and his father rebuilt it from the frame up. It was the only solid evidence he had that Cam gave a shit about him. His gift aside, he still knew better, but the bike had been something he could look on when he forgot that Cam just hid everything deep.

After this, he owed Davey big time.

The Wrench just turned away from both truck and captain and headed inside, his head still shaking and hanging a bit low, no doubt worrying what the repercussions of this fight would be. Lance stayed where he was, turning back to the truck and its load. The door was nothing—they could bang that out good as new—but the bike.... He drew aside the tarp covering it and his gut went sour as he took a long look at the wreckage.

With the extent of the damage—every inch of the bike appeared bent, shredded, or crushed—Lance knew the Knucklehead needed a complete rebuild before it would be street worthy. It was a reason to look up Cam that might just get Lance in the door, but the entire time he would know his father's torment; something else to hold against the Court fae.

Lance forced down a fresh surge of anger and reinforced his shields.

There was a hell of a lot to be laid at the feet of the High Court and damned if Lance wouldn't take the fight to them, if they kept it up. Bad things could have happened on the road today...if it had been another biker that had encountered the gremlin as Lance had...if the foe had been something above a spastic elemental, as next time it very well might be. Maybe the fae saw this as personal somehow, but if they did, Lance hadn't invited any of it. He kept out of Court politics, stayed away from any fae not one of his own. He had never thought he would rate such attention from the Court, but where else could this have stemmed from? Even had the encounter with the *Dubh Fae* not already implied such, gremlins were never so focused, so full of vitriol. There existed a love-hate relationship between a biker and the road, kind of like that between a cowboy and a half-broken bronco. When the ride was good, it was like a choreographed dance; when the road got temperamental, it turned into a battle for dominance. On occasion, the biker got a face full of asphalt. Other times, the biker ate up the road; but always...*always* there had been respect between the two. Lance ran a hand over the broken wing patch, tribute to his own serious wipeout...the one involving broken bones and a two-week hospital stay. There would always be some danger in any ride. That only made the challenge worthwhile.

What happened today was something altogether different.

It ended here. Time for the Wild Hunt to take the fight to the enemy. The Court needed to learn what a bad idea it was to mess with him and his crew.

Lance turned and went inside, his left side protesting each step.

The place was quiet tonight. A few bikers leaned against the side wall, watching a game of pool; a couple of local folk perched at the bar. No sign of Suzanne, though, or Gavin. At a table near the door, Tilly sat playing with someone's keychain. Lance gave her a bit of a squeeze and brushed his lips across her hair. She looked up with a brilliant smile but her focus remained on the shiny metal and the colorful bob they hung from. He chuckled and moved on past to the bar.

"Hey, Kel," he greeted the woman tending bar that night. "Gavin call in yet?" Earlier, after he had spoken to Delilah, he'd sent his lieutenant Underhill to find out who had painted a target on Lance's back.

"Sorry, nothing yet." She tapped two pints and slid them down the polished bar to those waiting. Lance's gaze followed the precision slide before coming back to her and the true question he wanted to ask. "Where's Suzanne?"

Concern darkened Kelly's china-blue eyes as they flickered up toward the ceiling. Lance's gaze followed, and he felt his temper heat up again. *Delilah's* had a second story split into a couple of apartments, accessible by a stairwell in the back room. One of the apartments was Delilah and Jon's place; the other belonged to Lance, his home off the road. He shared it with Suzanne, when she'd let him.

"She's been up there all...day," Kelly finally said. Lance caught the hesitation, but wasn't sure what to make of it. " 'Lilah takes up food once in a while. Mostly it comes back."

Lance wanted something to hit. Hard. Each day Suzanne withdrew more from the world, a timid miss where once she'd been a wildcat. On the surface, the *Dubh Fae* and his minions were to blame, thanks to fae politics Lance and his crew weren't even a part of, and had no desire to enter into. But all that had changed.

The Court is going to pay, he vowed silently. *Soon.*

Across the room, Tilly started slamming the keys into the scarred wood surface in front of her. Her shoulders twitched as she pounded the table in time to Lance's pulse and the tingle in his fins. His jaw tightened as he realized he was to blame. Ever since the encounter with the *Dubh Fae*, Lance's subconscious control wasn't worth shit. He forced himself to throttle down on his emotions before he set her off worse. Purposely he focused on his love for Tilly and willed in a bit of calm before giving it a push in her direction. The tempo of the banging smoothed out, then stopped all together.

Lance turned to Kelly with an apologetic twitch of his lips. He headed for the door to the back room without breaking stride. "Call me when Gavin gets here."

Kelly nodded, her focus already on the next drink order.

Taking slow, deep breaths, Lance concentrated everything he had on appearing unruffled. He projected thoughts of love, peace, and security. He did not stomp on his way up the back stairs and he did not let loose the glower tugging at his brow.

He must have projected plenty hard, because Suzanne stood on the landing at the top waiting for him; her eyes held shadows despite the well-lit stairwell. A faint tremble rippled through her. Maybe it was just him, but it seemed as if she might launch herself down them to reach him quicker. Lance lengthened his stride, taking two stairs at a time. "I'm coming, angel." He was a few steps from the top when she'd had enough waiting. Just in time, Lance braced himself and grabbed the handrails on either side. Even then she rocked him back as her legs wrapped around his hips and her arms clung to his shoulders. Bracing himself didn't help. The moment she squeezed he drew a sharp breath and fought the need to swear the stairwell blue.

"Easy, easy," he murmured instead, the pain only slightly ghosting his words. Despite the fierce ache down his left side, he wrapped his arms around her and climbed the rest of the way to the landing. He leaned his face into her hair and breathed deep. The wild, faintly woody scent was all Suzanne, never having seen the inside of a bottle, but underlying it an acrid sting pinched his nostrils as if someone had plucked out a hair. Fear. And not just the kind she'd felt for the past week that had her flinching from shadows and sudden movements, but a fear for him. Lance sensed the difference. Someone had told her about the wreck. When he found out who, they were going to skip having words and get right to the tune-up.

For now, Lance made soothing, nonsense sounds and gently rubbed Suzanne's back with both hands as he walked her down the hall to the open door of their apartment. By the time he'd set her down on the kitchen counter her shoulders had relaxed, and he spied a glimpse of his lady lurking in her eyes.

Suzanne ducked her head and leaned against him like everything was alright again. "Hey, babe," she murmured, her hand tracing the muscles of his chest. She wouldn't meet his gaze. There was a blank spot where she sat as he called on his gift to scan her. She blocked him. Like that was a surprise. It wasn't doing either of them much good; Lance still knew what she'd been through, what lingering effects the experience had had. Bound up tight the way they were, the scars would never fade.

He leaned back and touched his fingers to her chin, gently raising it.

"You gonna let them win like this?"

Her head jerked back and up, her eye swirling with anger, but still the shadow remained.

"You think I haven't tried to shake it? You think I want to be up here like some prissy little stupid *girl?*"

Even without his empathy, Lance knew that wasn't so. He just kept silent and let her rant, let her get it out, though even that wouldn't be enough.

"I'm afraid to ride, I'm afraid to get on my bike when it's just me and the road and whoever comes up behind me that I can't *see.*" She shuddered and he started the gentle rubbing once more.

Sounded simple, but it wasn't.

"So, you don't ride solo for a while," he said anyway, "until you're ready to ride on your own. It's not so bad." She growled and glared at him for the mere suggestion. No surprise there; surely that was one of the reasons they weren't together in a more formal manner—he kept trying to take care of her. Anyway, clearly there was more. He knew that, but she had to get everything out; she had to say it, fight it. On her own.

Frustration crackled in her words and across the surface of her skin until he could almost see it. He tried to reach out, to soothe her with his gift, but she still blocked him, more than familiar with the tactic. She made an effort to come clean. "I can't catch a glimpse of...anytime I see...." Her eyes squeezed shut and her head fell back as the panic reared up from wherever it hid to ambush her. Apparently, she had trouble even saying it.

She couldn't fight the panic attack and him as well. That quick Lance locked his hands onto her shoulders and, as carefully as he could, eased past her failing shields. He couldn't take away the fear and panic, but he did place himself between her and the flood, just until she could shore herself up. She tried resisting him at first, stubborn as always, but gradually the shaking stopped. The whimpers died away. Her breath came at something resembling normal speed. Lance lifted her down from the countertop and carried her to the beat-up couch in the main room.

Most of what she'd already said made sense. Only time would take care of it, but the part that tripped her up...*that* he needed to know. Until she got past whatever triggered this she'd never heal.

"What, darlin'?" he spoke softly by her ear. "What's doing it?"

She stiffened against him and a wave of embarrassment crested in her. He sensed she was too weary to be tough. Turning away, she pressed her cheek against the arm of the couch, instead of against his chest. Whatever she muttered was muffled by the upholstery.

"Didn't catch that, Suzanne," Lance let impatience edge his words; put a bit of the Club Leader into his tone. It was what she needed. Besides, he not only wanted her well because he loved her, the club needed her well, and soon.

"Red," she growled back, swinging out of his lap and up to her feet, looking as if she wanted to tear someone apart, and he was handy. "Just seeing friggin' *red* flips me out, okay?"

Lance held back a curse, bad enough his woman suffered like this, but to make matters worse, red was his favorite color. There were only a few shirts in his drawer that he could wear without setting her off. He'd have to make time to go buy more.

Suzanne's voice dropped low. "It's like they're watching me. I can feel them, but all I see is the red."

To anyone else that would sound like paranoia. Lance knew better. Blood formed a bond; the maledight creatures could very well be waiting for another chance. If they were, Sue would be able to sense that through the bond, no matter how they tried to mask themselves. But even if she was only experiencing an unhealthy dose of phobic paranoia triggered by the color red, that alone made riding impossible. Heck just walking around would be an issue. Red was everywhere. No wonder Sue had been so withdrawn. Of course, now that she'd 'fessed up they could work it out. And suddenly, Kelly's earlier hesitation made sense.

"You've been up here all week solid, haven't you?"

She didn't answer him but her eyes flickered up to glare from under her lashes. God help the *Dubh Fae* if Lance ever got his hands on him again.

"Oh, darlin'...." Lance stood up and wrapped his arms around her, ignoring her less-than-receptive stance. "You know you're safe here; they couldn't make it past the guardian wall without setting off the bells, and every rider in the place would be right there to jack them up."

Suzanne nodded, but it lacked conviction.

Lance tried again, this time going for a lighter approach. "And Mongo has Garm with him in the kitchen, so you know they won't make it in through the back."

Mongo did all the cooking at *Delilah's*. Garm, his massive wolfhound, kept him company. The dog didn't like anyone—especially magical anyones—that he hadn't been introduced to. His shaggy grey-black coat was crisscrossed by thick, old scars and his gaze was distrustful toward nonmembers. He made a particularly effective guard dog, contrary to the breed's typical friendly nature. Suzanne was a special favorite of the hound. "Can you say 'doggie treat?'"

Suzanne chuckled and relaxed a bit against Lance, brushing an easy kiss across his collar bone as she nuzzled in, her hand faltering only slightly as she swept over the road rash down his arm. They were, apparently, back to where she'd missed him. Before he could pull her back to the couch, the phone in his pocket rang. Groaning, he leaned his head against hers. Every time they had a moment together something pulled him out of it. He was tired of walking away from his lady. Instead, he kissed her hard and fast, and then a second time, gentler, trying to ignore the call. A pale version of Suzanne's usually throaty chuckle escaped as she slowly pushed him back. She was right, dammit. Lance let her go and pulled out his cell. It was Kelly.

"Think you can take coming down for a while?" Lance asked Suzanne before answering the call. She visibly shored herself up, then nodded, and he flipped open the phone.

He didn't bother with hello. "Yeah, we'll be right down."

"What have you found out?" Lance slid into the booth where Gavin waited. Suzanne continued past on her way to the bar, where he heard her ask Kelly for wings and a beer. Good. Eating was a good sign. Satisfied she was doing at least a little better, he drew his attention back to Gavin, who still hadn't answered.

For a moment longer Gavin remained silent, and Lance watched his eyes, recognized as the fae mentally shuffled and weighed the information he'd uncovered. "They're afraid of you, bro."

"You think?" Lance let a little sarcasm slide into his voice, then filled Gavin in on his encounter with the gremlin.

Gavin's lips quirked up in the faintest of wry smiles as he went on with the information they hadn't known. "You're gaining too much power. It unsettles many in the Court."

"Power? What power? You're joking, right?" But Lance knew his lieutenant was nothing but serious. "I've never even been to Court...or Underhill, for that matter. What kind of power could I possible have that would threaten one of the Faerie Courts? I barely have magic...they *are* magic."

The look on Gavin's face bore a faint resemblance to those he'd given Lance in the past—before the crossroads. It was a look that said, 'are you really this clueless?'

"Lance, do you realize exactly how big this club is? And I'm not even talking chapters; I mean the mother club, those who hang with you? Who *follow* you?"

Lance just gave him a look of his own. 'Get on with it,' this one said.

"This club would be nothing without the Wind Walker, and they know that Underhill. They track what you do and where. They are uncomfortable with the number of fae that run our colors, and there isn't a halfling biker in existence that doesn't ride with us. Then there's our name...they think it a threat that we are called The Wild Hunt."

"Oh, come on!" Lance cut in. "What? Did they run out of things to be bothered about, they have to manufacture something now?"

"My friend, do you know what they call us?"

Lance worked his jaw and felt his expression go hard and cold. "Abomination?"

Gavin nearly laughed, but too much unease tinged the sound for it to ring true. "We are called the Halfling's Court, out of earshot of the High King."

A chill crept across Lance's shoulders. Gavin was serious... and he was worried. Lance didn't blame him. He cursed himself silently. He should have paid more attention, but he had never been part of the fae world; what was left of his fae kin had always preferred the mortal realm. "Why didn't we hear of this sooner?"

Gavin's shoulder lifted slightly. "None of us bother with the Court. Few of us even go Underhill, these days."

"So, I have the High King of Faerie and his entire Court gunning for me?"

"No. Officially, they acknowledge nothing of your political power," Gavin answered. "They know nothing of the other changes...yet." His shoulders tensed as he went on, flexing as if he really wanted to unfurl; he wouldn't though. Delilah didn't allow it in the bar. Too disruptive, not to mention half the club might see it as a challenge. "The *Dubh Fae* was one of the fringers, tolerated at Court, but never much in favor. He and others like him sought to change that with their little plot. Now, thanks to the other day, he's outcast."

The mention of the Black One had the effect of a tripwire. Both men drew back from one another; they glanced over at Suzanne, who sat across the room with Tilly pretending she wasn't spooked by the guy in the corner in a red trucker's cap. When they turned back to one another, Gavin clearly waited for him to lash out. Lance merely signaled for one of the waitresses.

"Hey, Pat," he spoke low and easy to her, though no one missed the electric buzz of tension that lit his eyes and leaked into the air. He paused a moment as his gaze drifted back to

Suzanne. "Do me a favor; go ask Lyman for his hat, and then tell Delilah we have to get rid of everything red for a while. After that I need you to clear the back room and have Kelly ring the meeting bell."

When the waitress left, Gavin spoke up again. "Twice they underestimated your abilities. They will not make that mistake again." He sat forward, getting even twitchier as his muscles tensed, the image of a biker spoiling for a fight. Lance just shot him a look until he eased down.

"It's time to call a full Council. All Four Winds and the captains and lieutenants of all the Chapters...whoever's not already here because of the Stampede, get 'em here day after tomorrow...no excuses. Tell them to alert their Chapters to be ready to roll, war wagons and all, within the day." There was a smoldering glow in Lance's eyes, and his expression was hard set. "For now, get what you can of our own riders into the back room. We have some plans to make."

Lance rose and turned to head back there himself only to come face to face with Suzanne. He didn't need empathy to read the fury kindled in her eyes. The backhanded slap to his arm kind of gave that away. She was the only one that could get away with that.

"What?"

"What?! What do you think 'what?'" Suzanne's eyes glittered with annoyance, burning away some of the shadow that had worried him earlier. "Cut it out! Stop trying to coddle me. How am I getting better if you just rid my little piece of the world of everything red? You going to take out the traffic lights too? Maybe repaint the stop signs green?"

This was more than just a pale shadow of his lady. The spunk of her response crinkled Lance's eyes even as it brought a grin to his lips. "Now *there's* my Sue,"

She growled and whacked his arm again. "I mean it! Cut it out! *I'll* take care of this, got me?"

Lance just laughed, his hands raised in surrender, and called out to Pat, "Darlin', go ahead and give Lyman back his hat." He then reached out an arm and drew Suzanne to his side. "Come on—time for Church."

Bubba

Chapter Four

It was late. The impromptu meeting was long over, and the Wild Hunt's lieutenants had been sent to collect the Winds. The rest of the Hunt went off to find their own trouble. A couple members still sat at the bar, joined by some of the locals who had drifted in. All were calm, the atmosphere of *Delilah's* more than proof against any outside concerns—at least, for the short term. Lance stood in the doorway to the back room and just let all of it wash over him: the smell of bar food being served, the soft murmur of voices from the far corner, the gentle ringing of bells on the guardian wall as one of the waitresses headed out for the night, leaving only Kelly behind the bar.

Just like any other night. Hard to believe—taking in all that was as normal—that Lance had the fae equivalent of a bounty on his head. He took a deep breath and let the last lingering tension out of his shoulders. It was time to call it a night. It was time to head up those stairs and take up with Suzanne where they'd left off earlier. Only, as he turned he found his way blocked. The stairwell door stood open and his uncle, Jon, waited silently on the bottom step, elbows resting on his knees and his expression resigned.

"Gotta talk, son."

Now, coming from Jon, that actually sounded natural. Not pleasant, but natural. "What's up, man?" Lance asked, his tone and the set of his shoulders deceptively casual.

Jon shook his head and climbed to his feet. "Not here. 'Lilah's waiting for us upstairs." As his uncle spoke, Lance remembered the bell still in his pocket; Smear reacted with particular violence at Jon's voice. Lance just planted his hand on his pocket, stilling the tremors. The gremlin was a pain in the ass, but Lance still hadn't figured out what to do about it.

Tension again took up residence in his shoulders and up his neck. The bell was bad enough, but this unexpected conversation promised worse. There wasn't much in his life that Delilah had felt the need to discuss in private. Good. Bad. Every single praise or setting down she'd ever served him had been out in the open, didn't matter who was standing by. If past experience was any measure, this was going to be a whole other level of bad.

His uncle climbed half up the stairs before Lance started after him.

"Wait." He caught up and gripped Jon's arm. The fae stopped, half-turned, and gave Lance one of those lazy looks that wasn't really. Lance ignored it. "What's wrong with her?"

Jon blinked, then gave half a grin, his eyes a bit warmer than they'd been a moment before. "Nothing, I promise. This one's all about you."

That didn't sound a whole lot better, but he let go of Jon's arm and followed him up the stairs, moving past his apartment to the other. Lance walked in not knowing what to expect. Nothing seemed off. The smell of dinner mingled with the perfume of some roses on the counter. Lance stepped around the clutter of biker gear piled by the entrance and moved into the apartment proper. Delilah was nowhere in sight. He could hear music playing softly from the living room, but it clicked off as his uncle closed the door. The silence had weight.

"Delilah?" Lance called out.

She stepped into the arch leading from the living room. His aunt looked tired, a little stressed, but otherwise okay. Lance let himself relax just a bit. "Hey," he greeted her as he stepped forward and hugged her. She returned the squeeze, and placed a kiss on his cheek, but backed off in a hurry, turning to lead him into the room. Settling on the edge of the couch, Delilah stared pointedly at them until they sat down as well, Lance across from her in Jon's recliner, and Jon beside her, on the arm of the sofa. She then pulled something from her pocket and rolled it quickly from hand to hand before placing it on the table.

Lance snatched it from the table before he even realized the impulse. His fingers quickly closed around the trinket as if his aunt or uncle might take it away.

A ring. It was a tiny, delicate ring. Crafted of impossibly intricate knotwork: a stylized doe wreathed in rowan leaves of white gold, eyes embedded with gemstone chips that Lance could not identify. It looked like a fancy wedding ring. The moment it touched his flesh his body jerked and his chest seized, his last breath trapped inside. If he hadn't been sitting down he would have fallen to his knees.

His mother had worn this ring.

He felt her...her arms around his shoulders and her soft tears upon his head, followed by the whisper of a kiss. And then the feeling faded away. The moment passed and the air rushed from his lungs. His heart battered his ribcage. Suddenly he was freezing, trembling, and for a few seconds the sense of abandonment he'd thought he'd buried long ago surged. It was ridiculous, and he knew it. She hadn't left him; she'd died giving birth to him. Big difference. But she'd still been gone. Still left him alone, and, in effect, taken his father with her. And all this time this ring—in some way a part of her—had been kept from him. The ring cut into his palm, burning him like a brand. Betrayal bit the back of his throat but none of his turmoil made it as far as the surface of his skin.

He did not look at his aunt and uncle as he pocketed the ring. Instinctively, he slid it into the opposite pocket than the one with the bell, which had taken up a continuous tremble that did not seem likely to be subside. Jon and Delilah did not protest.

"So," Lance said, his voice hard and so controlled it came out nearly flat. "We here to talk or what?"

Delilah sat back like she'd been slapped.

"Yeah," his uncle growled from where he perched beside her. He put his right arm around Delilah, drawing her against his hip. "So take your head out your ass, because you're gonna want to hear what we have to say."

Lance didn't flinch, but he felt his uncle's disapproval. So much had happened in just a few short weeks and he'd let it get to him, walling himself off from those that cared about him. Now if that didn't play right into the enemy's hand, nothing did.

A glint of white gold on his uncle's right ring finger caught Lance's eye. Jon now wore a band similar to the one in Lance's pocket, only masculine. Thicker, heavier, with a stag instead of a doe...not a wedding ring, then; wrong hand. Odd. In all the years the couple had raised him, Lance had never seen that ring before. As far as he knew the only thing his uncle had retained from his life Underhill was an ancient dagger, heavy with scroll-work and magic. Clearly that was wrong because that ring reeked of the faerie court. Curious....

Lance met his aunt and uncle's gazes, gave a little nod, along with an apologetic smile. "Sorry, 'Lilah. What's up?" The last he directed at his uncle.

"Couldn't risk givin' that to you earlier." As Jon spoke he reached down to take his wife's hand, holding it up for Lance to see. "You wouldn't have been able to touch it, and you couldn't have kept it safe."

"Holy shit!" Lance half rose, his gaze locked on his aunt's red, blistered palm. As he watched, Jon lifted the hand and literally kissed the damage away. For the first time, Lance felt the current of his uncle's magic as he worked the healing, first one hand, and then the other.

"But you've...changed recently," Jon went on, as if uninterrupted. "You need it now to replace the protection your human nature used to provide."

"What do you mean?"

"When your human side trumped the fae, you were shielded from notice. You don't have that anymore."

"Well it wasn't precisely working before that, was it? Or did I imagine the *Dubh Fae*?"

"That's not the same thing; they weren't after *you*, just the halfling captain, there's a difference. Now, take the ring out of your pocket," his uncle ordered.

The gang leader in Lance bristled at his uncle's attitude, but he hauled back on the reaction and cut it down. Time to man up and stop letting his emotions get out of hand. Lance did as his uncle instructed.

"Now slip it on to the third finger of your right hand."

A short, sharp bark of laughter escaped Lance on that one. He looked down at the delicate ring resting on his palm—half of him expected the area to redden and blister any moment now— and then back up at his aunt and uncle. "You're kidding, right?" The band was so tiny he doubted even Suzanne could slip it on. Hell, it would be a shock if he could even get the top of his littlest finger through. His mother must have been beyond petite.

"Do it." The guardian bell shook a bit more fiercely in Lance's pocket as his uncle snapped at him.

Jon hardly ever lost patience with anyone.

Lance locked gazes with his uncle and shot one eyebrow up, but he listened with no further objection; his eyes still on Jon, Lance brought the ring to his finger, tried to ignore the fact that it was about the size of a child's, and pressed it against the tip of the finger he'd been instructed to place it on. An odd sensation traveled up his finger. He pushed, expecting the cool metal to press hard into his flesh, and instead it felt like his finger slid through water just shy of hot enough to burn. As the ring settled into place, the bell in his pocket abruptly fell still. He barely noticed as his gaze dropped to his hand and he swore in wonder. The ring sat comfortably at the base of his finger. Then there was a sharp pain, as if a thousand needles pricked his skin. The knotwork lines blurred a moment before coming back into sharp relief, and the gold glowed bright red, like it drew off his... He tried to yank the ring off, but it held fast, getting tighter the more he tried to shed it. Wonder turned to shock. Any moment he expected the still-constant heat of the metal to intensify until his flesh burned, the pain to increase until the finger severed. But neither happened; the pain faded, as did the bloody hue, though the gold retained a hint of red. The smallest part of his thoughts realized the doe had become a stag and oak leaves now mingled among the rowan, the rest of his attention locked on the fact that he couldn't remove the ring, no matter how much force he applied.

"What the hell, man?" Lance jumped to his feet before he even realized it, legs spread, arms tense, and his center of balance leaning slightly forward, ready for a rumble.

His uncle's chin dipped in response, as did his brow, every plane of his face hardening like steel in disapproval. Flashbacks from his teen rebellion years kaleidoscoped through Lance's memory. The look on his uncle's face: way too familiar. It featured heavily in those flashbacks, as did the ass-kicking that generally followed on its heels.

Before Jon could get to his feet, Lance shook off his aggression. Pure instinct fed the reaction, ramped up by everything going on. He throttled it down. This wasn't the time to get into anyone's face. For all intents and purposes, Jon and Delilah were his parents, not his aunt and uncle. They were the last people that would harm him. Settling back on the edge of the chair, Lance took a few deep breaths before speaking again. His voice remained tight with the tension still lacing his system, but he kept his tone civil: "I don't understand. Please explain."

"It's a 'Blood band," Jon answered. "A hereditary...artifact spelled to protect its wearer. It's bonded to you now and can't be removed short of death."

His uncle looked as if there was more to say, but if there was, he wasn't talking, though it looked like he wanted to. His jaw tensed and an eyebrow twitched, his eyes briefly met Delilah's, then the impulse visibly passed and he merely said, "You're going to need it...."

And then they told him about his birth, and the curse that took his mother's life, though he sensed they still didn't tell him everything.

The Fatboy outside still needed some skin, but the leather and chrome were clean and sound and the sixteen-inch solid wheels looked brand new. Gavin ran his eyes over the cycle as he approached the house but kept his hands to himself. The bike was going to be real cherry when Bubba was done with it.

As he approached the front door he couldn't help thinking the phone would have been quicker, simpler. That was the problem with all things having to do with the fae—and he should know—simple never cut it. This was a declaration and Lance needed the message sent loud and clear and as obvious as possible. It was fine to pick up the phone and call the chapter captains, but the Winds, they had to be summoned. So lieutenants rode out—one for each Wind—all of them flying their colors like a red flag in front of a bull. Lance had even convinced Jon to open portals to North and West, for those distances too far to get there in a day. And if that didn't send up a fireworks display worth of flares to the High Court, nothing would get their attention.

Bubba was the South Wind, one of the five founding members of the Wild Hunt. He went by the handle of Bubba or, more rarely, Nur, but neither was his name. There was a story there, but Gavin had never had the balls to ask.

Feeling as if he should be wearing battle armor, not bike armor, Gavin rapped on the aluminum screen door. The front door stood open beyond it, but there was no one in sight.

"Yo, you collecting coupons again, pretty boy?" The voice came from the side of the house. Turning, Gavin spied a mountain of a man in worn blue jeans and a black muscle shirt stretched over an impressive girth. In one hand Bubba held a two-pronged barbeque fork and the other gripped a beer. His hair was shaved close to his scalp and there was a rough patch on his forehead in the spot Eastern mystics labeled the third eye. As always, Gavin's gaze gravitated to that spot. Bubba was not his kind, but his nature spoke of magic and otherness. Something to do with that rough patch of skin...Gavin pushed the thought aside and brought his mind back to business.

"Not a road agent in sight today, Bubba. Got here free and clear and even kept it under megatron."

Bubba scoffed. "Yeah, not by much." He turned away, calling over his shoulder as he went. "Well, come on, I'm not standing here bullshitting while my porterhouse burns."

Gavin's mouth watered as he followed. When he rounded the corner of the house, Bubba had already slapped another steak on the grill. It stood out bright red and bloody next to the four others already there, the marbling still creamy white. The sound of sizzling was a siren song. Gavin swallowed a groan. The last thing he wanted to do was tell Bubba there they didn't have time. He cleared his throat anyway.

"What?" Bubba turned a shrouded glance in his direction. "You don't really think you're gonna interrupt my dinner, do you?"

Gavin did groan then, as Sammy, Bubba's wife, came out the back door. She had the typical delicate features, tip-tilted nose, and wings, of her pixie nature. The wings she mostly hid behind a glamour. Her hair was bright red and pulled in two tails atop her head. He knew for a fact she had the temper to go with it, Gavin spied a glimmer of that in the warning glance she gave him. In one hand she had a six-pack of beer, in the other, a plate of foil-wrapped food items Gavin could readily imagine as his mouth watered.

It wasn't getting any easier for Gavin to say it: "There isn't time."

Before he could go on, a ruckus sounded from inside—banging and swearing and just-changing male voices talking trash as only brothers could. All of that stopped the moment Zack and Shawn hit the doorway and spied Gavin standing there. He braced himself instinctively. Shawn, though lean, had the raw, barely bridled energy of his mother, and if Bubba was the mountain, Zack was the foothill, smaller, but still powerful enough to break the unsuspecting. Gavin visualized setting roots deep into the solid earth. It's all that saved him.

"Wingman!" they cried as they tumbled out, the screen door clattering behind them. Seconds later they slammed into him. Laughing and grinning as if he was Christmas and birthdays wrapped into one. He laughed back and gave them each a hug before shooing them out into the yard.

When Gavin turned back he caught both Bubba and Sammy giving him the eye.

He sighed. "It's a War Council."

That brought a frown to Bubba's already intimidating expression. "Who? Not the Red Dawgs again, is it?" While the Red Dawgs had been an on-again-off-again problem for the Wild Hunt, Gavin wished he could tell Bubba yes.

He shook his head.

"W*hell*...usually they're the only ones stupid enough." Sammy spoke up this time. "Who's trying to prove themselves now?"

Gavin had to agree, the club in question was better known among the biker crowd as the Dumb Dawgs, but no.... "Dair na Scath."

Dead silence. For just a moment Sammy looked like someone smacked her in the back of the head with a board, then her eyes grew fierce and her cheeks flushed. There wasn't much room for talking between the pixies and the fae of the High Court; Sammy and her kind went right for scratching out eyes any chance they got. From the looks of her, it went a bit more personal between her and the High King, even.

Bubba himself looked beyond pissed as he stood in front of his grill. There was definitely some history there, Gavin would stake his originals on it. For a moment, the barbeque fork resembled a weapon in Bubba's hand. Any illusion of soft edges on the mountain hardened.

"Shit." Gavin backed up a step.

That seemed to register with the South Wind more than anything. He closed his eyes, breathed deep, and snapped his head from side to side until the cartilage cracked.

The edges softened again, but when Bubba's eyes opened, they burned lava hot.

Gavin heard a sizzle followed by a pop, and before the South Wind turned away, Gavin could have sworn the rough patch ignited. A fleeting hint of El Niño hung on the air despite the season as Bubba lifted the grill top. Before Gavin knew what happened, the picnic table was set for five with perfectly grilled porterhouses and all the trimmings. "Eat up, we've got road to haul."

Gavin didn't waste time arguing.

Gort

Chapter Five

"Boy, what're you into now?"

Lance just stood there, hip shot, trying not to glower from beneath his brow. Here was the one person in the world that never seemed impressed, the one person that should have loved him and taken care of him, no matter what, and he was practically a stranger. Most people didn't even know Cameron Cosain was his father, even less actually knew him by his full name.

In the club or outside of it.

Heck, the man didn't even look old enough, hardly. His hair was thick, golden brown, and the only wrinkles on his face came from squinting in the sun and riding bare-faced in the wind. His eyes, now...those were old.

Lance understood why, but that didn't really help at the moment; he was too raw. With serious effort, he shook off the resentment. He didn't want to hate his father, and if this was the only way they could be close, it was up to him not to screw it up. It took effort, but he smoothed out his expression and gave a rueful smile.

With a tilt of his head, Lance gestured toward the back of the house and Cam's workshop, where Davey had dropped off the Knucklehead before fleeing the scene. The wreck served as a convenient excuse for coming out here. Not as important as warning Cam, though. Only, Lance had no clue how to bring up the subject, so for now he stuck with the bike. "Need your help." His muscles tensed more with each step as he strained to hear the sound of the screen door slapping wood behind him. They walked out back in silence. Lance braced as they rounded the side of the house, knowing what Cam's reaction would be....

"Aw, Che-*rist!*" Cam's fingers shoved through his hair.

...Because that was pretty much how Lance felt too.

"What the *hell* did you do?" The words came out angry, the tone aggressive. Lance's lip curled in reaction, even though he knew his father's anger masked fear and concern. Knowing that didn't help much.

Until his father spun around.

For a fleeting instant, and perhaps the first time in his life, Lance recognized in Cam's eyes the sheer terror the man had learned to hide from his son's empathy. The ghost of Lance's mother lurked in that gaze along with a memory Lance barely understood; the reason why his aunt had pretty much raised him. As Cam looked him over for mortal wounds, Lance wanted to hug his father and tell him everything was okay, but that would be a lie. Not with the whole friggin' faerie court gunning for the Wild Hunt with Lance as target number one. For once in his life he couldn't honestly say Cam had nothing to worry about.

Instead, Lance kept his voice low and neutral, saying, "Can we fix her?"

The redirect seemed to derail his father. He stilled and glanced back at the Knucklehead. " 'S gonna take some work," he answered, hand rubbing his jaw before wiping over his eyes and back up through his hair. "Have to scour the bone yards hunting sound parts, I'm thinking." He went into the workshop and came out with a tarp. With care and gentleness he never dared show his son, he drew it over the cycle and secured it, offering what protection he could to the bike's broken bones. Then he turned to Lance and stunned the crap out of him.

"Inside."

He pointed toward the house.

The invite soon made sense, though; the moment they crossed the threshold it felt like entering a dead zone as the protections on the house kicked in. Shields covered the whole property, but not like this. There was some serious shit guarding these walls and everything in them. Cam didn't have a lick of magic, so the shielding must have been the work of Uncle Jon...or...Lance's mother. And for the first time in his life that he could remember, Lance was allowed back inside.

The place felt odd. And lonely. No pictures hung on the walls and nothing personal lay about. No mementos...no sign of family...Cam existed all alone, inside his house, and his heart. Lance got it; Cam kept no connections with anyone he stood a chance of losing and thanks to the circumstances of Lance's birth, that's precisely what Cam expected to happen. Only the death of Lance's mother had affected Cam so deeply, he didn't just distance himself from his son. The more Cam was likely to care about a person, the more he shoved them away, as if his presence in their lives would cause their death. He even rode as a lone wolf rather than wear the colors of the Hunt or any other club.

"What the hell were you doing?" Cam snapped again, right up in his face, quashing the moment of understanding. Lance's muscles bunched in reaction and his eyes narrowed. He had to keep reminding himself this was Dad. His father went on, oblivious to the warning signs, hand gesturing sharply in the direction of the back yard. "And how the *fuck* did you walk away?" A thin thread of awe ran through Cam's tone in spite of the outrage radiating from him.

That last comment startled a chuckle out of Lance. He'd lost some skin, and a little blood, collected a few bruises, maybe, but yeah, standing on two feet and breathing unassisted did seem something of a miracle, now that he thought about it. He pulled the guardian bell from his pocket and held out his hand with it resting in his palm, waiting for it to dance by itself. The little bugger seemed disinclined to cooperate. The little shit. Or...could he have fallen loose? Lance tipped the bell up, checking to see if the magic still trapped Smear inside. Two bright-red eyes glared out at him, but the gremlin remained still.

"Son, what's wrong with you?"

"Nothing, I'm fine, Cam," Lance answered as he reached across with his other hand and picked up the bell by its ring, tilting it until the gremlin glared at his father.

The startled confusion on Cam's face was priceless.

"Meet the newest assassin of the High Court...retired." Lance gave the bell a shake and could almost half hear the gremlin scream. "Second strike, actually. The first happened two weeks ago, a closet halfling trying to make brownie points with the High King." He filled his father in on the details of both encounters, but didn't mention what happened to Suzanne or his own transformation. Cam played at being distant, but he had his trigger points. Even though Lance couldn't feel his dad's emotions through the walls he'd built up a minute tic at the corner of Cam's eye betrayed him. Lance pretended not to notice as he went on. "Thought I better warn you; if the Court has decided I'm a threat, they could decide that makes you fair game."

A bit of heat crept into Cam's gaze. "Wouldn't be the first time."

Lance gave a sharp nod and they stood there in an awkward silence until Smear screamed once more, even louder than before. A whack against the edge of a nearby table silenced him.

"You should get rid of that."

Stubbornness bubbled to the surface as Lance dug in his heels. "It's mine," he grumbled, and gave it another whack. "And he can't have it." Even to his own ears he sounded like an ass.

Cam gave him a look of disgust. "How old are you? Give me the damn bell; I'll take care of it."

The bell disappeared as Lance's fist closed around it. He couldn't help himself; the impulse to resist took over like a compulsion. The pewter surface burned cold against his skin, though it should have been warm enough from being in his pocket. Cam might have been right, but that was beside the point.

"*Now*," Cam ordered. "You'll get it back when I'm done." Lance held his gaze for a moment, and fought whatever had a hold on him. It took an effort, but he managed to drop the bell into his father's hand.

Cam nodded and a moment of warmth passed between them before the awkward silence settled back into place. Lance cleared his throat and suddenly Cam turned away, busied himself opening up an old steel thermos and dropping the bell inside, before screwing the cap on tight.

Yeah, alright. "Catch you later, *Pop*," Lance called over his shoulder—his father hated being called Pop. Lance pulled his cell phone from his back pocket and headed for the front door. He'd told Delilah to expect a call for retrieval; he might as well wait at the curb until someone came to get him.

"Hey, Son," Cam called out. Lance stopped and half turned just in time to catch the set of keys arcing toward his head. "Take the Panhead," his father told him, referring to his back-up bike. "At least for now; gonna be a while before we can get to the Knuckle."

"Gort! Gort!" The High King of Faerie bellowed as he stormed through the bough-crafted corridors of *Sidhe na Daire*, his Underhill stronghold. His link to the trees carried the cry until the place echoed with it, sending lesser fae scattering. Gort would have heard, regardless; with ivy woven through the crown of every oak but those of Dair's own bower, the High King could have whispered and still been heard by his druidic advisor, yet the toad had yet to answer his summons. Dair traveled halfway to the corner of the realm where Gort had long ago taken residence before the fae in question appeared.

Slight for even one of the fae, Gort stood youthful, like a sapling, surrounded by the sculpted forest giants that ringed a wide clearing along the corridor's path. In form, he was as slender and long as one of his ivy vines, his hair and eyes the deep, dark green of those same leaves aged by many seasons. Dair snarled to see him standing there calmly—smugly?—as if he hadn't betrayed trust; it bore noting that the betrayer stood well into the sunlight, beyond the reach of the oaks' shadows. *Yet, not far enough beyond*, Dair thought. A sly smile played about the monarch's lips. With an upward flick of his wrist he awakened the wide-spread roots of the ancient trees. A rumbling shook the earth as those shallow roots stirred, then thrashed, sending Gort to his knees where the long, pale roots whipped up and lashed about him, trapping the druid in place.

Confusion and distress darkened Gort's eyes even further. He did not struggle. He did not rage. He was too canny, surely, to behave so, caught in grips as he was. "Sire, is aught well?"

Dair merely stared, his gaze as hard as petrified wood. He circled the druid, watched him closely and read the signs of his body and the frantic wisps of almost-thought that escaped the druid's control. He came forward and pinned Gort with a glance that did not waver: "There was a child," he said, his voice the deep and disturbing murmur of oak boughs before a storm.

Gort paled and went very still. Something indefinable shifted deep within the trapped fae's eyes.

"You did not tell us there was a child."

"Pardon, sire, what child?" Gort asked on a sighing breath, pausing as the retaining roots tightened on Dair's command.

"Tonight, we felt a binding, druid," the High King said, the words deceptively controlled and even. "*Her* band merging with another...bound by blood; now *tell us* of the child."

"You said they were dead to you, the lines of blood forever severed; the dead bear no children. I abided by your will."

"A child of the royal blood raised up by mortals and outcasts and you claim to abide by our will?" Dair's voice dropped to a harsh whisper, "Who is the father?"

Silence. Stillness. Like the hard grip of fear.

"Who?!"

Again a shifting in Gort's gaze, emotion too deep and controlled for Dair to name it by sight, the lips smiled though, all compliant and eager. "I do not know, sire, but I will learn all I can, if you bid me...."

"If we *bid* you? You will bring us all knowledge on the matter before the sun sets again or we will *bid* you die!"

Dair had a doubt: Gort's loyalty now lay in question. He would be a fool to place faith in the druid. Instead he stirred the magic of his realm, imbued it with his will, and unleashed it. The root released with a whiplash, the tip opening a gash in the druid's cheek, trailing beads of blood like glittering, amber-tinted sap. The smallest sliver of oak embedded itself in the wound, mingling unnoticed with ivy. Gort's head nodded quickly, but not sufficient to hide the emerald flare of anger in his gaze.

"Sundown," Dair reminded sharply as he turned and stalked away, already immersed in his own thoughts. His daughter-wife was dead, the ring passed on. Somewhere in the mortal world there existed a child of his blood, Anaiphal's child, some outcast's get, no doubt. Perhaps a female of the royal line that would bind him further to the throne—as her mother should have—that none dare ever again question his rule. He glanced down at the band on the third finger of his right hand, a skillful crafting of white gold knotwork...a stag wreathed in oak leaves...but no matter how masterfully wrought by his own hand, it lacked one key element.

Goddess help him should a rival ever think to test its protections.

He pushed the thought from his mind and reached his senses toward the oaken splinter he had left in Gort's wound, testing the link with Gort still in his presence. His advisor's breath became a peculiar echo as it filtered through both Dair's ears and directly into his mind.

Dream

Chapter Six

THE DOOR AT DELILAH'S OPENED AND THE SCENT OF HOT dust and burnt rubber wafted in. Lance shifted on his stool until he faced the entrance and then leaned back against the bar. First Gavin stalked in looking as burned up as he smelled, then he seemed to vanish as a silhouette in the doorway blocked out most of the natural light: Bubba—massive, immovable, and limned by a corona, much like the sun during an eclipse. He slowly stepped forward and the door swung shut, leaving most to wonder if they'd imagined the effect as the tint on the glass muted the light from outside.

"You made good time," Lance greeted them and gestured to Delilah to get them each a beer.

Gavin growled and stalked closer, right up into Lance's face. Lance just stared back from beneath hooded lids.

"You owe me new tires," Gavin forced through a jaw clenched tighter than a good girl's knees. When Lance just nodded, his lieutenant grabbed the longneck and swigged half the brew down as he headed across the bar in the direction of the men's room.

A low, rich chuckle brought Lance's attention back around. "Causin' trouble again, Bubba?"

The mountain cracked a smile and lifted his brows, suddenly looking like a cheerful elf, only super-sized and in blue jeans and a patch-covered leather vest. If Lance hadn't noticed the flame in his eyes Bubba would have pulled off innocent as well.

"He was whining that we were taking too long, so I took us a short cut."

Lance just shook his head. Bubba was a fire elemental. They'd ridden together often before Lance stopped his wandering; he could readily imagine Bubba's 'short cut'...and the results. Slagged tires were not beyond reason. "Nur, this is serious."

"Damn straight it better be," The South Wind drawled, not even blinking at the use of his chosen name. "Sammy had off tonight...."

Lance gave him a rueful smile. "Sorry, bro, but we're in for a serious throw-down."

"Yeah, I figured," Bubba said, the cheerful façade sliding from his face. He slipped a wad of cash from his pocket and counted off four one hundred dollar bills—the cost of some nice, high-end tires—and laid them on the bar. Lance grinned at Bubba and nodded in understanding.

Bubba picked up his beer and took a draw before looking in the direction Gavin had disappeared. "I better go calm down Wingman before this party gets started."

As he turned and walked away the door to the bar swung open once more letting in a sudden stiff breeze and a lean, dark-haired rider in beat-up blue jeans and a leather jacket heavier than he was. His features held a faintly Asian cast everywhere but in his strong jaw and cleft chin. Enlil, the East Wind; better known as Blow. He headed right for where Lance lounged against the bar. Before the door closed behind him a hint of static crackled the air, followed by a *pop*, like the air equalizing—at least, for those with enough magic to feel the change. Blow stopped where he stood and his gaze locked on the door to the back room, as a short, stout figure walked into sight. Solid and steady, with a wild thatch of hair all the shades of red and brown and gold, Enki, the North Wind, stepped into the room, his cleft chin thrust forward, leading the way. He had a weathered face and muscles that rolled and dipped like a range of hills. Typical enough, he went by Rock. Both Winds drew within feet of one another and stopped. The atmosphere crackled as earth met sky.

If it wasn't for their matching scowls and their chins, Lance thought, *you would never know they were brothers.*

As if they could hear his thoughts, both rounded on him and growled. "Half!" they snapped in unison, then glared at each other for it. Like their Sumerian namesakes, each had a problem with the other; probably more than half the reason the elementals had chosen those names for themselves when Lance brought them together to form the Wild Hunt. Actually, all four of them had chosen names representing their element, but in this case, both Enlil and Enki showed an appreciation for irony, particularly when it came in such fitting symmetry.

"Behave, children," Lance said, leaving his stool with an easy move of power and grace. He was all leader as he approached the Winds, ready to break heads if they didn't stand down. Before anyone had time to react, the static came back, followed by another *pop* from the back room. Every eye went to the doorway, though only a few actually felt the arrival. An Amazon stood there. Tall, lean, and mean, in molded leather armor and a foul mood. The West Wind had just blown in, and she put El Niño to shame.

This one everyone called Dream, as in wet, though Lance suspected no one clued her in on that. They had too much respect for the ease with which she could kick their asses. If she suspected, she'd never mentioned. She'd chosen the name Anatu for herself, which meant water spring. Not coincidentally, it was also the name of an obscure goddess of war. Right now, she stalked forward, her gaze traveling the room as if she expected to find the threat already among them.

"Down, girl," Jon murmured from behind her. Lance had almost missed his uncle leaning against the doorframe looking wrung dry. He sounded hollow. "It's all good here. 'Sides, the old lady'll be miffed if you trash her bar."

Before the words had left his mouth, Delilah came sliding over with a can of Red Bull in her hand. As she passed Anatu, a rumble sounded deep in her throat, ominous, and—coming from her—much more threatening than any growl. The West Wind merely dipped her head the slightest degree. More acknowledgement than deference; still she stepped back and her posture eased.

"Here, sugah," Lance's aunt said as she held out the can to her husband. "You look like you need a pick-me-up."

Jon smiled. "Why sure...." Delilah yipped as he stooped and wrapped his arms around her hips, with very little effort lifting her up. "*Mmmm... just what I needed....*" He buried his face against her shirt and pivoted until the two of them disappeared through the doorway.

"Move along now," he called over his shoulder. "Nothing to see here."

Lance chuckled and turned his attention back to the Winds. That quick, the humor left his expression. "Behave." These were the charter members of the club, they ran their own territories, but they were on his turf; that made him big dog.

They fell into step behind him as he headed for the center of the room, his eyes scanning the crowd. Over a hundred bikers and a few unaffiliated patrons filled the place. Lance signaled to Kelly behind the bar. Nodding, she reached up and smacked the brass bell hanging over the register twice. The music stopped, as did all conversation.

"Okay, folks, closing time," Lance announced to the crowded bar. "Anyone not wearing Wild Hunt colors needs to leave. Now." The regulars got up without a word, left cash on the table for their tabs, and waved on their way out the door. One or two outsiders looked like they would dispute the call, until the Hunt's enforcers stepped forward, arms crossed over chests only marginally less impressive than Rock's, with considerably more height and reach. Grumbling loud threats on their way out, the outsiders vacated the premises.

Tilly hurried to the door behind them, concentrating intently as she flipped the lock closed. It was one of her daily tasks and she took it very seriously. Her job done, she then rushed across the bar to wrap her arms around Lance, her face flushed and her lips grinning. "Good job, Dumplin'," Lance murmured against her hair as he hugged her back. "Now go on and sit by Sue." He gently set her aside and gave her a little push. Even the Winds smiled at her innocent joy in his praise.

Everyone loved Tilly.

All the soft expressions faded as she sat down and Lance walked to the open center of the bar, where on rare occasion dancing nominally took place. He waited until the Winds dropped back to lounge against the bar and Gavin and his other lieutenants came to stand by his side. Lance laid it on the line, recounting the recent attacks for the captains of the other chapters and anyone else unfamiliar with what went down. He stared into a lot of hard looks, noted the gleaming eyes of those looking forward to the fight, but they needed to understand the stakes.

"Dair na Scath's got a grudge, folks, and he's playing nasty," Lance wrapped up, his gaze locking with each of the riders. "This isn't a turf war; it's about power. The High King of Faerie thinks I'm a threat, and that means he and the Court think the club is a threat. They're gunning for us. Doesn't matter where you go; it's likely to be open season on anyone running Wild Hunt colors. They've tried for me twice now and only got kicked in the teeth for it."

Cheers and stomping went up, mostly from the mother chapter. Lance let them go on a moment before holding up a clenched fist.

Silence.

"So far the fae have targeted only me and mine; doesn't mean they aren't going to escalate...."

A hiss interrupted Lance. It came from the far corner of the room where a member of one of the support chapters stretched the length of one of the extra-long booths, one leg cocked and his bandanna pulled over his eyes. "It's already started," he called out as he hauled himself upright, pushing the bandanna off of eyes barely able to open for the swelling. Black circles surrounded them. Lance flinched as he got a look at the man's mashed nose and the amount of skin he'd left on some stretch of highway. "Who is that?" he murmured quickly to Gavin, who had taken role earlier as the bikers came in.

"Mitch Calhoun, called Irish," Gavin answered. "Rides with the chapter out of South Peak, Tennessee."

Lance nodded his thanks and turned back to the biker. "Go ahead, Irish."

"Caught a love nudge just outside of town, some loco wearing Red Dawg colors. Sent us into a skid I couldn't pull out of, right into a brick wall. You can see it banged me up pretty good...sent my old lady to the ER. They're holding her overnight."

"You said it was a Dawg?"

"Yeah, but that ain't quite right," Irish answered. "Got a bit of the Sight from my Mamó...nothin' much, but enough to know something rode the dude harder than he was riding his hog."

Lance met the man's gaze and nodded again in thanks before turning to the gathered members. "Anyone else?"

As other members shared the details of additional encounters—some involving the Red Dawgs, but others more inexplicable—Lance waved his uncle over. "Can you do anything for him?" he asked, gesturing toward Irish.

"Some," Jon answered. "One way or the other...not a lot of juice left after all I've done this day." He stepped behind the bar, hauling out a med kit to rival any field medic's—along with some components they would never have known what to do with—before weaving his way through the crowd to where Irish sprawled once more. Lance turned back to the general discussion, bringing it to an end with another closed fist. "As you can tell from what you've heard, we're not just talking skin and steel here...they're coming after us with everything they've got and that means big-time magic. You need to warn your riders, and your families.

"Those of you that need to get people out of harm's way, arrange it yourselves if you like, or see me after, and we'll work it out." Several bikers shuffled closer, as if queuing up. One or two others sneered as Lance went on, clearly not taking him seriously. "Make no mistake...The faerie courts have just declared war on the Wild Hunt. You stand with us, be prepared for some serious shit.

"You want out, check your colors at the door, but know this...you'll never ride with *any* club again, my word on it."

He gave them a moment. None looked away as Lance scanned the crowd; none tore the colors from their leathers and left them in the dirt.

With that out of the way, Lance introduced the Winds and the captains of each chapter, then his own lieutenants, as anyone not able to reach him would then call them. After that, they settled down to form a game plan. They bandied ideas, but for the most part, they had no choice but to wait and see, not knowing what to expect from their foe. Lance issued a few final instructions: members were to ride out in four-man teams, no one going solo; no splitting lanes or riding two-up, and everyone was to check in for now, and be ready to grab their gear and bunk down in the barracks-style compound Delilah maintained behind the bar for War Councils and more peaceful gatherings.

"Everybody clear?" Lance asked. It wasn't really a question.

Many nodded, or even grinned, more than ready for a knock-down fight.

But the fae, to the last one, offered Lance a salute he did not recognize, though it both disturbed him and sparked a deep sense of satisfaction he couldn't explain. From the corner of his eye he caught a stunned look on Gavin's face and heard his friend murmur the words on all the fae lips: *mo urraim, mo tiarna.* My honor, my lord.

The words hit Lance with the power of an invocation. He felt it with every sense he had, the five God gave all men, as well as magical and empathic. Then the humans took up the cry and it struck Lance as hard the second time as the first. Though most of them could not know what they spoke, it carried as much conviction as from their fae brothers' lips. At the forefront stood Irish, his eyes fierce and open wide, though both were masked by the yellow-green of a fading bruise.

"Damn," Lance murmured beneath his breath, the word drawn out as he began to wonder what exactly he'd taken on.

It was midnight. Bubba's wife, Sammy, and their two boys had arrived by one of his "short cuts" an hour ago smelling pleasantly of hickory smoke. They'd sacked out upstairs with Suzanne and Tilly. Downstairs, Lance and Gavin sat at the bar. The Winds played poker at a corner table, and Delilah sent Kelly home with her guy and a couple of friends, taking her place at the tap, though there wasn't much call. Jon had gone out back to make sure those bunking in the compound had what they needed for a somewhat comfortable night. With everyone more or less settled or getting settled, there were no more distractions. Lance's thoughts drew back to the salute like a dousing rod to water.

"What happened here?"

Gavin shifted on his stool, hands throttling his beer as if it would disappear if he didn't. Lance waited patiently; they didn't have forever, but it was a good call they probably had all night. Besides, he wasn't completely sure he wanted to know. Whatever had happened felt profoundly life-altering. For all of them.

"Fealty."

One word really did say it all. It barely whispered off Gavin's lips. Even so, Lance trembled deep inside. If the Court hadn't been gunning for him before, they certainly would be now. A motor club was one thing; the oaths there were to the organization, not to any individual. Fealty—pledging fidelity and allegiance specifically to Lance—was a whole different thing. He might as well find a gauntlet to slap across *Dair na Scath*'s face, because like it or not the rumor of the Halfling's Court had just become truth.

Lance swore...not loudly, but with conviction. Before he could turn to face Gavin full on, two things happened: the front door opened, and every bell on the guardian wall set to ringing violently.

A thud sounded from upstairs as something roughly the size of a body hit the floor, but Lance didn't have time to wonder or worry. He and every biker left in *Delilah's* came to their feet braced for a fight. They'd expected the Red Dawgs, or a gang of magically augmented adversaries; they were confused by the tall, thin man just standing in the doorway. He had a vaguely punker look: a shag of dark green hair and piercing eyes, with just a hint of wary. There was strength in the lean lines of him, though not much muscle evident, and at his waist, just visible beneath his coat rested the haft of a dagger. He had his hands raised high, away from the weapon and palms out, while his shoulders slouched in the slightest defensive hunch. A fresh wound ran down the side of his face, crusted over, but still red and swollen; it ran at odds with the air of harmlessness he projected as steady as the Sunday matinee. The members of the Hunt quickly came together before the door to the back room, blocking it. The bells kept on ringing.

Delilah took a few steps forward and stopped with her chin thrust out, her hip cocked, and her arms crossed over her chest.

"We're closed." The fae—for fae he was, or one close to them—did not move except to nod acknowledgement.

"I bear a warning, madam, not a thirst." The fae's gaze flickered from Delilah and settled on Lance. His eyes widened and the breath visibly caught in his chest. He forcefully exhaled and bowed with just his head then slowly brought it up again, his eyes never leaving Lance's. Quite the trick—and it reeked of sincerity...not that that meant anything real.

Lance felt his lips quirk in a half-smile. So formal. Definitely fae, then. A true punk would have snarled back. Lowering his shields, Lance extended his empathic gift: fear, worry, pride, weariness, a deep, abiding strength, faintly flavored with a touch of bitterness, but nothing of a darker nature. He glanced toward Blow and Rock. Waving one hand, he sent them forward to flank the stranger, with the other and a bit of magic he stilled the bells. He then turned his attention back to the unfamiliar fae.

One step brought Lance forward even with his aunt, a second took him just past her. He gestured for the others to stay back, to stand between those upstairs and harm, then pinned all his focus on their visitor.

"I'm listening." After all, no use pretending: for once it really was all about him.

Before the stranger could speak there was the sound of someone pounding down the stairs, nearly falling on their way down. Then the door to the back room yanked open.

Suzanne stood there poised to strike, her knees bent and her expression a curious mix of fierce and frightened, but only because Lance knew what he was looking at. Sammy appeared behind her and tried to pull her back. Suzanne shrugged her off, her breath shallow and forcefully audible...kind of like an enraged bull, only petite. In one hand she brandished what had to be the meanest knife from the kitchen drawer upstairs, in the other she held a large steel tent spike, likely all she could find in the apartment. Lance moved to intercept her, though others were closer. What could he say? His natural impulse was to protect, though his mind wasn't too clear at the moment on exactly who needed protecting.

The knife in Suzanne's hand wavered. Confusion seeped into her gaze and her head tilted slightly, unconsciously, back and away. Panic shoved confusion out of the way. That was when Lance heard the pained gasp behind him, from the direction of the front door, and then something metal skitter across the floor.

"Ah, hell!" he swore, as he spun around standing between Suzanne and whatever was going down. He needed the women out of there and someplace safe. "Sammy, Delilah, get her back upstairs!"

Sammy couldn't man-handle Suzanne alone and Delilah didn't seem to hear him. She stood as transfixed as Suzanne, staring toward the front door where Jon had the stranger pressed against the frame, his ancient dagger at his throat. Blood trickled in a thin line beneath the high collar of his simple black shirt. The fae's blade had disappeared from its sheath.

"He's in danger," the fae spoke softly, with care, his eyes flickering from Lance's face down to the ring on his finger. His gaze fixed upon the ring, intent. He clearly spoke to Jon.

"Yeah, no shit." Jon's response came out a growl. "Thanks, but I'm about to fix that."

Lance swore with a bit more heat to it and took a deep breath, his eyes closed and his muscles bunching as he centered himself; too much happened at once and he'd missed half of it. He opened his eyes and spoke through clenched teeth.

"How about putting a hold on this, Jon? I'd kind of like to know what the *hell* is going on."

"Jonraphal thinks I've come to kill you," the stranger answered. "Or whisk you away to a worse fate, perhaps."

The blade pressed closer as he uttered Jon's true name. The name only two people in the room knew: Delilah and Lance. The name his uncle had left behind with the faerie court. "Who's the Citizen, Jon?" Lance asked.

"Gort," Jon ground out.

Both Delilah and Gavin gasped, so Lance figured that meant something, and not in a good way, but personally that didn't tell him shit. "Been friends long?"

The other fae spoke before Jon could respond. "Yes...or allies, at least, though Jonraphal may not see it so."

Jon brought his fist up, a sharp jab to the guy's gut. "Don't *ever* use that name again!" A bit more blood flowed from Gort's throat as his upper body jerked forward with the blow. Lance barely recognized Jon. Gone was the laid-back, gentle man that had helped raise him from the day he was born. Gone was the hard-assed Jon that kept the teenaged Lance in line. This Jon was cold and lethal. Murderous.

Time to intervene, before the situation got any worse; Lance moved forward, pausing beside his aunt. "You, and her, upstairs. *Now.*" he ordered. Brooking no arguments, he gave Delilah a nudge toward Sammy and Suzanne and watched until Gavin ushered them through the door, closing it behind him as he followed them. More thuds pounded up the stairs, then the apartment door slammed. Bubba and Dream moved to block the path to the back room. Satisfied, Lance stepped over to his uncle. Blow and Rock moved in synch with him, like well-trained bodyguards, their eyes never leaving Gort, freeing Lance to focus on Jon. He slowly pressed his fingers on the hand holding the knife. "Not like this, man."

His uncle shuddered, made a little chuffing sound deep in his throat. For a moment Lance thought he'd have to take him as the knife pressed just a little harder. Gort drew a sharp breath, and Lance felt the fae's desperation on the exhale. Then the moment passed and the tension eased, allowing Lance to grip Jon's wrist, drawing it back away from flesh until he could get a look at the damage. The point had barely pierced the skin in a shallow, angled cut leaving a bit of blood and a hard, pale line where the blade had been ready to slice deeper. With a disgusted sound and a hard expression molding his features, Jon jerked his hand out of Lance's grip and stepped back. He did not move far, and the knife remained in his hand.

"Gort is advisor to the *Ard Rí,*" Jon spoke. "You know...the one that's gunnin' for us...."

"I am your kin, Jonra...*Jon,* though distant," Gort responded, again in the same formal tone, though Lance's uncle hadn't spoken to him. "No matter what my position." He turned to Lance and went on, "Yours as well. So know this, what he says is true, on both accounts...but also know the High King's desires are not my own.

"The post was most...advantageous, allowing me access I might otherwise not have had, access used to safeguard one whom I cared for deeply." The fae's eyes softened, and then saddened, as he turned to consider Lance, glancing at his face as if looking for something he wasn't sure he'd find, then looked down at the ring newly set upon Lance's finger. "Your mother."

Lance's empathy read only regret and sincerity. His mage sense detected no sign of glamour meant to cloud the senses or foster deceit. But could his senses be trusted? He was still finding his feet again, magically and empathically. He glanced at the Winds and gave a little tilt of his head. It was a familiar gesture among the five of them; each of them shook their heads, letting him know they sensed no magic, which they were particularly sensitive to as elementals. Nodding, Lance turned his attention back to Gort and quietly considered the fae with all his focus. The guy made him a little uneasy. Lance wasn't too sure he cared for him, but he couldn't pin down a reason for it, so he made a judgment call; "Okay, patch him up." He directed the order to Jon, not altogether certain he would follow it. "The rest of you, lock everything down. We don't want any more...surprises while we hash this out."

While the others closed up, Lance stepped off to the side a moment. Pulling out his cell phone, he fired off a text message and waited for the reply, which came back quick. Satisfied, Lance pocketed the phone and started flipping chairs seat-down on top of the nearby table. As he moved to lift the one in the corner, he discovered Gort's blade on the floor. Jon must have tossed it across the room when he'd disarmed the other fae. Picking it up, Lance slipped it into his boot sheath before continuing his task.

In short order, they'd lowered the blinds, put up the chairs, cleaned the taps, and wiped down the bar. They all worked quickly and efficiently because Delilah would have their asses if they did a sloppy job. Everyone stopped mid-task, though, as a few minutes later a key turned loudly in the back door lock. A rumbling growl and the scrabble of thick claws on ceramic tile sounded from the back as Mongo and Garm came through the kitchen door.

Mongo would have been huge...if Bubba hadn't been in the room. Garm still was. And if the dog hadn't been leashed on a stainless steel, half-inch anchor chain he would have gone for Gort's throat.

There was no barking—Garm couldn't anymore, thanks to a particularly vicious scar that wrapped his throat like a collar—but that didn't stop the dog from plenty of growling and chuffing and further scrabbling of claws, this time on expensive hardwood, as the hound fought against the chain. Gort went still. Even the others looked stunned at the particular vehemence of the dog's response. Lance just strolled past them to the door leading to the back room. "Okay," he called over his shoulder, "now we can talk."

They all filed in, Gort conspicuously escorted on all sides, wounds reluctantly healed by Jon, all but the one the fae came in with, which had already scabbed over. Mongo and Garm trailed in last, settling on the bottom step of the stairwell leading upstairs, rather than sitting at the round table in the corner with everyone else. The cook leaned back and closed his eyes seemingly to nap, the dog's chain looped around his wrist, while Garm settled at his feet to stare intently at the fae.

The silence—as most are—was uncomfortable. The room stifling. The scents of blood, tension, and loathing nearly overwhelmed Lance. Bad enough being trapped down here sorting the mess out, instead of upstairs with Suzanne, without trying to hold his breath the whole time and sweating his nuts off. "Blow, take care of it." There was no need to explain.

The East Wind closed his eyes, drew several deep, chest-expanding breaths, then several more until it seemed that his breath fogged with condensation more in line with a brisk October night out under the stars. He held the last, largest lungful of air. And held it. And held it some more. His eyes slowly opened, reflecting the pale, faded blue of an autumn sky. He exhaled slow and steady. On his breath flowed the crisp, cool scent the air held between Halloween and Thanksgiving, just before the snows crept in with their sharp bite. The temperature of the room dropped in kind, cool and comfortable. When he was done his eyes darkened back to their usual warm grey.

Lance nodded his thanks then turned to the others, his gaze circling the table until it locked on Gort. "Get talking, or I'm going to bed and the others get to decide what to do with you."

Gort looked toward Jon, rather than at Lance, his expression taut with new fear and old pain as he spoke, his gaze never wavering and his voice solemn. "He has learned there was a child."

Jon swore viciously in several languages, both mundane and otherwise, and pushed to his feet.

Now, were they talking about him, or Tilly? Could have been either, technically, though Lance got the impression they meant him, given the looks both of them shot his way. The Winds didn't even pick up that much, judging by the perplexed puckering of their brows as they glanced from the three of them then at one another. As one, they stood, but only Dream spoke: "Looks like this is more personal business than club business," she murmured as the others nodded. "We've got your back, Dušan, but for now we're going to move over here and give you some space to have it out."

"Let us know when you're ready to talk battle plans...or garbage disposal," Rock added in a deep, quiet voice as he pulled a well-worn pack of cards from his pocket. With that the Winds moved off, heading for a table far across the room.

Lance grinned grimly and shook his head before turning his focus back to the two fae. "*Who* learned?"

"Your...." Gort began.

"No!" Jon cut him off.

The grin went away as Lance carefully considered his uncle. "*No?* Care to explain?"

"I cannot," Jon said. "I'm oath-bound."

Lance didn't like the answer. He respected his uncle and understood the fae enough to know the all-importance of oaths, but this was serious shit. He shoved to his feet and snarled, "Who!?" All eyes were on him except for Jon and Gort's. They held their own silent communication eye to eye before Jon looked over at Lance with something haunted in his gaze. "*Dair na Scath.*"

Gort scowled. "He would not even know if you'd held back the ring, if you had not bound the boy. Until then he was not even sure she'd passed."

"Boy!" His father called him that. Lance didn't like it then and he sure as hell didn't now, from a stranger. He had long left boyhood behind and was fast losing tolerance for the fae messenger.

"I have five centuries, *boy*," Gort snapped as if his own patience with the situation had finally been exhausted. "How many have you?"

Before Lance could set him straight, Jon cut in, confusion running through his words, "He truly did not know? How?"

"A bit of timely distraction when you'd fled…a bit of applied will after, constant and steady, until gradually he could no longer sense either of you. I could do little enough to protect her, but I could do that, though in the end it made no difference. I did not know of the curse."

Skepticism and respect warred in Jon's expression, along with an overall air of puzzlement.

Lance looked from fae to fae and felt his jaw clench and his brows dip. "So he knows I was born at some point…somehow I think he'd already clued to that. What's your point?"

"He does not know you are the child. If he knew of *whom* you were born, who both your mother *and* your father are," Gort answered, "he would have killed you long since, well before you ever had a chance to be a threat."

"So, what…he's playing catch up now?" Lance scoffed. "Tell him to bring it on!"

"This is nothing to mock, *Prionsa*."

Jon hissed at Gort's use of the foreign word. It somehow seemed familiar to Lance, but he had no time to track the memory down as Gort went on. "Now he wishes to crush your power, not slaughter you. If he discovers your lineage, his goal will change. He will increase his efforts a hundred fold."

"Yeah, well, he can only kill me once, assuming he can pull it off at all."

"And how many others as well, to get to you?"

Lance scowled at that and sat forward more aggressively, holding Gort's eye as he spoke. "He won't find any of us an easy mark. Hell, he couldn't even get the job done before I knew he had it in for me; he won't stand a chance now that we're all eyes-up."

"Before you represented an annoyance, now…much more. He has sent his champion to deal with you." Gort's eyes then flickered to Jon and back again. Something played at the edges of that gaze, but Lance couldn't place it; a flicker of intent impatience at odds with the emotions evident empathically, as well as in the fae's speech and posture. The moment passed and the conversation went on, but Lance remained alert as Gort continued to speak.

"I am afraid the *Ard Ri* is going increasingly mad. He used to rule well, and justly. But since the death of his queen, and...."

Jon growled a warning and Gort clearly modified his statement.

"Since the death of his queen and the events stemming from it, he took forceful measures to maintain his rule. His care for our people has turned into an obsession with power. Underhill is twisted with this perversion." Worry laced Gort's words as honest care and passion for the fae world sang clearly through him. "The lesser fae resist. The high fae simper and indulge as it suits them, while doing as they please outside his influence, further corrupting the foundation of our land. Many have left altogether, forsaking Underhill even as you have. The very framework of our society continues to crumble the longer he sits on the throne. The land sickens beneath his feet and he can no longer feel it. His hold is precarious and will not stand against a rival of even dubious origins. If he learns the truth he will not stop until you are ended."

"So, anyone with sense is fleeing Underhill, those that have not are twisted, and I have a crazy king after me who sees anyone associated with me as fair game, right? And for some reason I shouldn't know why? It's not like I would have expected anything different anyway."

"Can you protect him, as you have before?" Jon asked Gort.

"It is too late for hiding."

Lance leaned forward and pinned Gort and his uncle with a glare. He was fed up with secrets and whole conversations going on like he wasn't there. He'd have a little talk with Jon when all this was over about whatever his uncle kept from him. For now Lance settled for putting an end to their talking over his head. "As if I would hide anyway; forget about me...I'm a big *boy*...what can you do for my people?"

"A simple charm, perhaps, to warn them when the fae are near; another to shield them from notice, where I can," Gort said. "Not much beyond that, though, and only for those most at risk.

One hundred, no more. I do not have enough power to safeguard them all."

Jon made a startled sound at the number and when Lance glanced at him he looked impressed. Lance hadn't had much to do with magic so he couldn't quite feel the same. All he knew was that they had to do better than that. "What about the other fae; those in the Hunt?" Lance directed the question at Jon. "Can any of them provide some kind of safeguard for those that need it? Some kind of 'hide me' spell or something for those left unprotected?"

Jon considered, then nodded his head. "Some of them."

"Good, we get started on that in the morning then."

Across the room the wolfhound snored gently from where he curled on the floor at Mongo's feet. Both of them looked beat and Lance figured Mongo at least would have more than his usual load of work come morning. They weren't needed for the rest of this.

"Hey, Mongo," Lance called as he leaned back in his chair and stretched out, crossing his ankles beneath the table. "Naptime's over, man, time to go to bed." Mongo grunted and unfolded himself from the step. "Send my buddy Garm over here on your way out...I have an introduction to make." Mongo just grunted again and shook the anchor chain from his wrist as he shuffled out the door. Lance gestured and Garm ambled over, chain dragging; a second gesture and the hound nuzzled Gort's hand with much loud snuffling and a long lick of his tongue. Thus introduced, the dog then ambled out the door into the bar letting out a low, deep woof as he went.

Lance then raised his voice and called across the room. "Hey, poker game's over too. Come on over, Gort's going to give us the dirt on *Dair na Scath* and his goons."

Tilly

Chapter Seven

Anaiphal had born the Abomination.

There had been little doubt the cursed halfling was her get: when Dair had finally seen his rival's face through the link with his advisor, the shade of his daughter-wife's beauty had been clear in those rough mortal features. Then Dair heard their words as they spoke, resonating through the splinter of oak Gort unwittingly brought into their midst: Gort's confession of his part in the matter, the warning he bore; new betrayals compounding those of the past.

And yet, during their conversation, they did not give him the name of the one who lay with *his* Anaiphal. The one he must wreak vengeance upon. Gort's confession sent Dair to the chronicle trees, where the entire history was recorded for the royal line of *Rudha-an* and those that sat the throne. With magic and the strength of his fingers he tore at the bark the druid had spelled over the smooth surface of the trees. Tore it and shredded it until the writing lay revealed, until he uncovered yet more duplicity.

He stood before the wall of memories surrounded by devastation. Long strips of bark littered the ground. Sap pooled at his feet. White flesh laid bare, scored and scoured until not one word of the betrayal remained hidden. He was unaware of the splinters beneath his nails. The smell of fresh, brutalized wood went unnoticed. In his blood he felt the trees screaming; himself, fury stole his voice.

The bark had not hid the unsteady steps of his reign.

The trees before him chronicled his daughter-wife's infidelity. Beneath protective bark he found the record of her outcast years. The last days of *Anaiphal na Rudha-an*: Her defiling. Her death. Her murderer.

Dair's face twisted and clenched and trembled with the strength of his wrath. First the eldest, Tilsaia, defied him. Then Anaiphal showed the same deceit. With the aid of her brother, she'd flouted Dair's rule and his decree, shunning the good of her people and denying the duty of her blood, as the other before her had. Anaiphal, daughter of the lines of Rowan and Oak, forsook the throne and despoiled herself with the touch and the seed of a *mortal*.

Dair stared upon the name of the man with whom she had betrayed him, whose murderous hands held her as she died giving birth to his spawn.

Cameron Cosain.

Dair whispered the name with venom. His senses rippled out across the mortal realm like a shockwave, like magical sonar powered by his hatred for that man. As it echoed back, his teeth clenched in a vicious grimace. He could sense the man, and with him the unexpected presence of the gremlin, but something turned aside the hammer blow of his will. Something familiar.

Protections somehow yet sustained by his Anaiphal.

Lance had a vague memory when he woke up. Warmth. A kiss. His own murmured protest as cool air invaded the spaces that once cradled warm curves. Suzanne's breath against his temple as she whispered, "I'm going downstairs."

He'd had the impulse to object but sleep had crept up behind him and dragged him back down. The last few weeks had exhausted most of his resources, and the rest...well, Suzanne had that to answer for. She'd tucked the blanket back around him and Lance had drifted off, unable to resist. Now the sun slanted in to tap against the outside of his eyelids. He groaned, then cursed as he threw back the covers and reached for his shorts, then his jeans, and put them on. Before standing up, he grabbed a pair of socks from the bedside table and slipped his feet into them, followed by his boots. The apartment was on the west side of the building. For the sun to wake him it had to be close to one o'clock, which meant he had to find someone to chew out—boots helped. Really. He didn't care how much he needed the rest, snoozing in bed wasn't going to keep the Court off their backs or make his people safe. Pulling on a faded red muscle shirt he headed for the door. On impulse he stopped by the dresser and drew Gort's ancient dagger from the top drawer (he might have decided to trust the guy, within reason, but not enough to arm him again). When Lance's hand touched the hilt he sensed a faint hum he hadn't noticed before, pleasant and enticing. The weapon warmed in his hand and Lance had the urge to slide it onto his belt for all to see.

Bad move. Stupid move. He resisted the urge, instead slipping the sheathed blade into his right boot. Dropping the leg of his jeans back into place, he left the room.

A faint whiff of coffee came from the kitchen along with the sound of banging. From the living room he heard *Star vs. the Forces of Evil* on the TV; it was a toss-up whether Tilly or Jon was responsible—they both watched the show whether the other one was there or not. Either way, Lance cringed. The show was a cross between an acid trip and a marijuana high. He glanced through the arch as he passed the living room.

He was wrong. Gort sat there on the couch, a bemused expression on his face as he looked at the TV, his head slowing tilting to the side as brain matter turned to mush. Lance spied a nest of pillows on the floor mere inches from the screen. Tilly had chosen the programming then, though she had abandoned her post, likely in search of food.

"I'd advise looking away now before you lose any more brain cells," Lance growled as he stalked on to the kitchen looking for the coffee. He found Tilly there pawing through the bottom cabinet where the cereal would be if she were in the right apartment. A tragic little pout bowed her lips as she looked up at him. A single tear rode down the curve of her cheek.

"No Crackle Puffs." She looked both devastated and extremely cute.

That right there put the pause to Lance's mad-on. He squatted down beside her and ruffled her tumbled curls. "You're next door, Dumplin', the cabinets here have all got different stuff in 'em."

Her expression morphed until it resembled Gort's, including the same little head tilt, and Lance's fists clenched. That he still had his cousin alive was a miracle, but to see her so changed. Every day they prayed for her to come back to herself. It was possible. The doctors had told them the reversion to a childlike state after a coma generally lasted no more than a few years. It had been five and with each day that passed it seemed more likely she might be one of the rare few for whom it never lifted.

Lance was back to wanting to break faces again.

He could see her mind trying to click but nothing quite lined up properly anymore. It wasn't so bad most the time, but it really got him when he looked into her face and could see a glimmer of whatever frustrated part of her knew she should understand. He took a deep breath of lingering coffee aroma and reined himself in. His hand slid into the curls running down her back and tugged her forward until he could plant a kiss on top of her head. "It's okay, sweetie, give me a sec." Lance pushed himself upright and reached into the cabinet high over the fridge, the one a person had to be *real* determined to get into. From the far back recess he pulled out his secret stash of Choco Puffs. There was a squeal and he had only seconds to drop his heels back down and brace himself before soft curves crushed against him in an ecstatic hug. He laughed and carefully set her aside before pouring a reasonable amount of cereal from the box into the bowl she already had waiting.

There was a sound from the doorway and Lance glanced up, his eyes narrowed. "*You* can't have any," he grumbled at Gort as the box went back into the cabinet out of Tilly's reach.

Lance himself grabbed a mug and poured in the sad remnants of coffee left in the pot. It would do until his mood grew civil enough to head downstairs for a cup from one of the fresh pots always available at *Delilah's*. Tilly munched happily at the kitchen table, her ear half down to the bowl as the Puffs crackled away. Lance took a moment to switch the tiny portable TV on the counter to DisneyXD for her. It would help to keep her occupied. Then, with a nod to Gort indicating that he should follow, Lance headed back to the living room and clicked off the mind-rot there.

"What's the deal here?" he asked as he settled into a battered armchair. Gort sat back down on the couch where he'd been when Lance had ventured out of his room.

"I was asked to play companion-keeper for Tilsaia." He gave a little shrug, as if to say it was not his place to question. "She pleaded me stay and I agreed. Her parents feel it is safer for her to stay above with the way things are."

Lance tensed and watched Gort closely. He set his mug down and leaned forward. "Her name's Tilly."

Gort nodded and glanced toward the kitchen. "Perhaps her familiar name, but with that face, that hair, surely her formal name is Tilsaia, is it not? She is the mirror image of *her*, though the eyes are more like Anai's." He seemed to consider it as if the matter were an academic puzzle. "Or did they name her Tilsari? It is, after all, a derivative. I can see where they might not wish...."

The way Gort went on pissed Lance off, both the rambling and the implications. What exactly was Jon keeping from him; they were going to have to have a long conversation. Soon. Lance would try and get what he could from Gort, only he respected his uncle too much to go around him like that. Lance would give Jon the chance to come clean first.

Gort must have spied Lance's expression. From the feel of it, it could not be an encouraging one. The fae's words trailed off as he absently rubbed at the scabbed wound on his face.

"Her name," Lance repeated firmly, "is *Tilly*. Remember it."

Maybe it was the light. Maybe it wasn't. For a fleeting moment, Gort's eyes seemed to flare a brighter green. But then it faded and Lance had to wonder if it had been there at all.

He pushed to his feet, the coffee forgotten, and aimed the remote once more at the TV. He was feeling particularly malicious as Star babbled back on screen in high-def color. "Keep playing...nice...until someone comes up to cut you loose." For the life of him, Lance couldn't figure out why Jon and Delilah had felt comfortable enough with Gort even after last night to trust him to ride herd over Tilly. She seemed fine with him, but

Lance didn't like it. It nagged at him like the feel of something caught in his teeth. No matter how much he went digging, it eluded him, though there was no way he should be able to miss it. An empathic probe of Gort revealed none of the emotions that often accompanied deceit or subterfuge, but something was off.

Lance took the stairs down to the bar two at a time, searching for Jon and Delilah. The remote went with him.

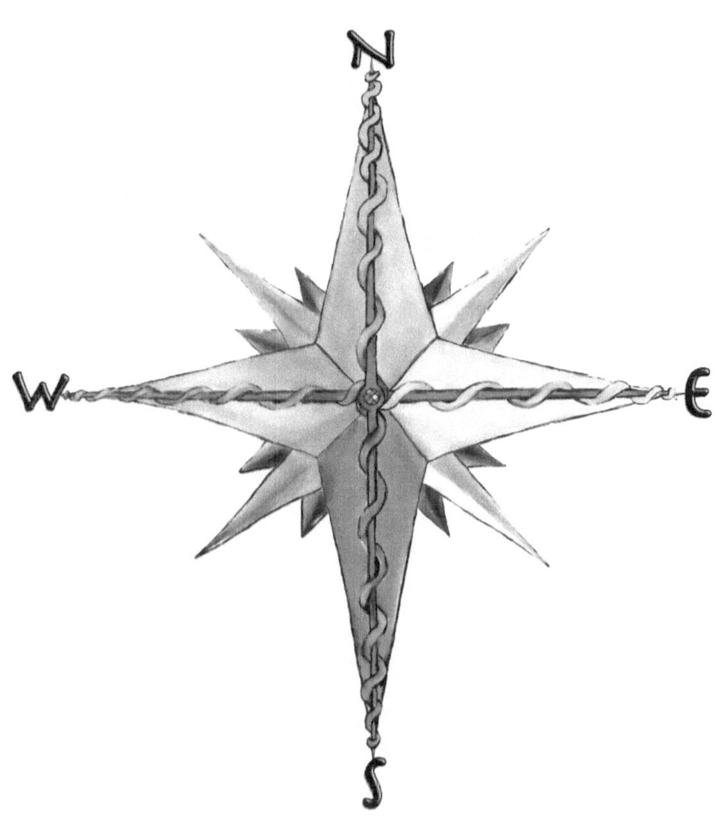

N
W
E
S

Kerwin
The Dubh Fae

Chapter Eight

THE SUMMONS WAS QUITE UNEXPECTED. KER HAD STRIPPED the bower of his belongings and had turned to leave when two heralds of the Court came through the entry. One bore a scroll, the other a globe-tipped staff. Ker braced himself; both against their presence and the sudden wave of contempt and disgust that rolled before them, though their faces remained impassive as any courtiers. The onslaught of emotion had him off balance, but he drew himself up and wrapped his features in a shield of indifference. It wasn't as if this was anything new; even before the *Ard Ri* revealed Ker's mixed blood, he had not been popular among the Court. They might not have known why he was different, weaker, less pleasing to the senses, but they didn't need to know why to look down on him. He hailed from a lesser line in their reckoning, and they clearly found him wanting.

As the humans so crudely put it: *Fuck them.*

"Well?" Ker demanded, all the laid back arrogance he could muster behind the word, though the urge to defend himself sent his right wing fin tingling and a sharp shaft of pain through the damaged one on the left.

With the briefest of formal bows—which nearly shocked Ker out of his façade—the herald bearing the official scroll unfurled it and read the contents aloud: "Kerwin na Bran is hereby summoned into the presence of the *Ard Ri*, Dair na Scath." Both heralds then bowed, a bare dip forward, and pivoted to the side, leaving just enough room for him to pass.

Curious. Very curious.

Ker considered them both. Then the message they bore. Technically, he no longer came under the rule of the *Ard Ri*, having been cast out of the Court. Of course, it would be fatal to test that theory now, while still upon the grounds. What had changed, that the High King summoned him? The heralds betrayed nothing in their manner. Curiosity won out, that and the logic that if the High King wanted him dead or imprisoned Ker would have merely been taken, not summoned. With insolent slowness, the *Dubh Fae* drew his bag to his shoulder and strolled through the gap, the heralds falling in close step to either side.

As in the High King's hall, the walls surrounding them were the close-grown trunks of various trees, here with the crowns interlacing overhead. Normally the branches were populated by will-o-the-wisps and luminous fireflies. It was telling the fauna had fled, leaving the route lit only by the sullen glow of foxfire under foot, and the mage ball balanced on the herald's staff.

None of them spoke along the way to the Hall, but the silence that encompassed them came from more than that; other than themselves, the path was deserted. Both creature and fae had withdrawn, leaving only tension and a sense of waiting to fill the air. Ker kept his breathing steady and calm, but the atmosphere pounded him as relentless as the surf upon the shore. He readied what defense he might need as they walked, just short of drawing magic to flood his wings.

When they entered the Court, Ker shuddered and nearly reeled. It was like slamming into a wall of solid emotion, un-controlled and roiling, like acid against the skin and a shout point-blank to the ear. Hatred. Suspicion. Rage. His vision dimmed, then darkened under the bombardment. It was chaos, madness....

Ker dropped to his knees, only at the last minute managing to turn the fall into a formal bow of extreme deference. By his reckoning, he was no longer bound by such things, but if it masked his moment of weakness, then let Dair na Scath think he fawned. As with the smoke of a fire, violent emotions rose to the highest point, Ker had learned. By dropping low he was able to clear his thoughts of the emotional assault that was so new to him. He shielded himself before he flowed gracefully to his feet, coming forward to stand before the dais and the High King.

Shock nearly sent him once more to his knees as he caught sight of the devastated chronicle trees closest to the throne.

He waited for Dair to speak.

And waited.

The king just stared, unveiled loathing in his gaze, and something more, something Ker could not conceive. Was it fear? It had been such a brief flash and this ability so new to him. He tried to probe with his fledgling senses only to have his mind impact with the mental equivalent of slamming into a cliff. Ker shook his head and with rapid blinks attempted to clear his vision. Only extreme control kept his expression neutral.

Dair na Scath, *Ard Ri* of the Faerie Courts, stood at the edge of the dais, eyes level with Ker's, his fingers splayed as if he would throttle him, if only it did not involve touching halfling skin.

"Attempt that again," Dair said, "and you will not survive the effort."

Ker lowered his gaze, nodding his assent. But, from beneath the shadow of his lashes, he watched the High King, and inside he sneered. In that instant before the slamming, he had seen what hid in Dair's most private thoughts. The reason the biker loomed such a threat.

"Would you redeem yourself, Kerwin?"

A snarl pushed against Ker's lips at the hated name—Little Black One—and the implication served with it. He suppressed the impulse ruthlessly and inclined his head to the High King once more.

"Good." Dair said, his lips smirking. "There is a man, mortal. He is an enemy of this Court and has imprisoned one of our faithful servants. You will retrieve the man for judgment, and bring us the vessel containing the fae." There was something more behind the matter. There had to be; Nothing about the charge seemed worthy of a halfling's redemption in the Court's eyes.

"His name?" Ker asked.

"Cameron Cosain." The High King held up a rough nugget of asphalt.

"You will need this," he continued. "It will guide you to our servant, held captive in the mortal's dwelling. Do this and you will prove yourself above your deficiency."

Ker ignored the insult. Instead, he cocked his head and considered the fae king. "And if I succeed?"

"You do not die."

The Black Fae drew himself straight to his full height. "And if I succeed?"

Dair did not speak; aloud, anyway. His eyes, however, spoke all too clearly of pain and suffering and lingering death meted out personally for the *Dubh Fae*'s impertinence.

Ker lifted one brow and met the eye of the king. He was already outcast and showing weakness would not preserve him if death was his fate. If there was anything he knew, Dair na Scath respected strength over weakness, even if he did not by any means encourage the former.

"If you manage not to *fail*," Dair spoke from the dais, "we will... discuss...your status at our Court."

"Your word?"

The king sputtered and growled. His high emotions struck Ker one sharp blow after the other. For a long moment, the *Dubh Fae* expected to die.

The moment ended.

"Our. Word."

Cam sat on a folding chair in his driveway, an oil-stained tarp spread out beside him on one side, the half-dissected remains of Lance's Knucklehead on the other. At his back sat a bucket that had already caught more than a fair share of unsalvageable parts he'd stripped from the cycle. It was a cool day, but acrid sweat darkened his shirt.

He didn't know how his boy had survived the wipe out; God knew the bike hadn't. Pushing the thought away, Cameron forced himself to focus on the music screaming from the radio and his continued task of removing and sorting parts, nothing else. One of the fittings gave him a bit of trouble. He reached for the WD-40 from his toolkit only to find it wasn't where it belonged. Climbing to his feet, he headed for the workshop. He found the lubricant on the far bench next to the crank case Jake had been working on the last time he was here. Jake was a local kid that just wouldn't stay chased away. No matter how many times Cam had run him off he came back the next free day to pester him. Maybe it was the kid's determination, or maybe it was the fact Jake reminded him of his own boy; whatever the reason, on occasion Cam gave in and let him stay a while, teaching him a thing or two as they worked side by side on various cycles, in remembrance of the good times with his son. Such moments of weakness would bite him in the ass one day, but he still couldn't help it. He'd been alone a very long time.

Grabbing the can, Cam growled and stalked out of the workshop, going back to his seat. His mood only grew fouler with each piece of trash he stripped from the bike. The task didn't absorb him enough to keep the fears and worries edged out of his mind—not with the bike serving such a harsh reminder. Cam had his reasons for keeping his distance from his son, and it wasn't lack of love or some bullshit idea that somehow Lance was to blame for Anai's death. No. Or, at least...not once the self-pity loosed its grip, courtesy of one of Delilah's well-placed verbal kicks and a smack upside the head. Not until the boy turned three had Cam been forced to cut him loose. There was no choice. He had no other way to protect his son.

A shudder went through Cam at the memory. He had to set what he was working on down as his hands shook. They'd been camping in the woods behind this place and the boy had wandered off Cam's lands. Cam had been chopping up deadfall for firewood when he looked up and noticed. The boy hadn't gone far, and he wasn't out of sight, but he'd moved outside the carefully crafted protections his Anai had set to safeguard their child when he came. She'd warned Cam the child's blood would sing out to the fae even if his mortal nature muted his magic—they hadn't known for sure. The fae half of his nature would remain a beacon to her kind. That alone would not betray who bore the child, but Anai had left a gift for him in Cameron's keeping, just...in case.

Cam could still remember her somber expression as she placed her hand upon his heart and whispered fae words into his ear. His chest had seized and he landed hard upon the ground, her palm still firmly in place, her lips still murmuring. It burned like fire and ice, a stiff wind and the dust of the earth converged within his chest, leaving him gasping. She whispered a final word: Done. Then she placed her lips upon his own and lifted her hand away. A jolt and his heart beat once more. She drew back and murmured "I love you" and he physically felt the vibration of her words within him. Again he heard the words as she spoke them:

"A piece of me for each of you," Anaiphal told him, a sad smile on her face, "should I not fare well in this."

"You're going to be fine, you're both going to be fine," he argued, panic fluttering in his chest beside that new tingling warmth he'd yet to get used to. "What if you need it? Take it back! It's all going to be fine."

Her smile widened and she shook her head at him. "What is done cannot be undone. Once gifted, it cannot return to me; only to those for whom it is destined. Half for you, and half for our son. A piece of me forever. You will never be free of me." Her expression grew mock-fierce with that last.

He groaned. "God willing, my faerie queen, God willing. Don't ever leave me alone! What..." his voice cracked. "What do I do? If. If I must?"

The fear won a little more ground. "I do not know. I do not know that this has ever been tried with a child not fully fae. With my kind such a gift would simply flow to the one meant to receive it at their majority..."

"Eighteen?" Cam asked, his expression showing the tight strain of trying to comprehend.

She frowned, forgetting the differences between their races and their times. "No, forty-five." Her eyes teared with distress as she realized how long her son would be without her should things go badly. "Or maybe sooner, if the bearer were near to death."

"Just..." Cam had to clear his throat to finish. "Just near to death?"

Anai nodded, her face pale and her eyes haunted. "If not before the last breath, the gift dies with the bearer."

The breath trembled from her and her hand smoothed at Cam's chest as if she needed the reassurance that his heart again beat strongly with a piece of her beside it. He knew how she felt.

Cam could not bring himself to ask, but he could not help wondering, what if the gift did not go to their son as it was meant to? Instead, he wrapped his arms around his wife and mate, tucking her safe beneath his chin as he crooned to her a lullaby his Grammy used to sing in the dark of night when Cam had still been afraid of the bogy man.

It was the dark of night for them.

And the bogy man was back.

His love had not warned him of the rest. But then, clearly she hadn't known what to expect. He closed his eyes against the memory, but it did no good.

The boy was not on unprotected ground as much as a minute when a swirl of leaves and dust formed up beside him. Unaware of the danger, his son laughed and clapped, pudgy little hands snatching at the leaves. A slender arm reached out from the swirling, bark brown but not as rough as that. It ruffled his hair and something laughed back with the rustling of wind in the treetop. The swirling stopped and a dryad stooped down, arms reaching to claim his son.

"No," Cam screamed, crossing the border of his land with his ax raised as he snatched away his son with the other arm, turning slightly away so his body came between the boy and harm. The dryad had hissed, then drawn back, her eyes narrowed. "Rudha-an!" she screamed and lashed out at Cam, recognizing that part of him that was Anai. The clawed hand did not score, but the dryad's eyes narrowed further as she glanced from father to son, an alien satisfaction curling across her face, her gaze calculating. She opened her mouth as if to bell, as a hound would, to others of her kind. Cam narrowed his own gaze and let loose the ax still raised above his head.

There sounded the thud of hard iron striking wood, followed by a shriek the likes of which Cam prayed he and his child never heard again. They crossed to their own lands without looking back, abandoning their gear in place. The boy bawled all the way home; Cam joined him with silent tears streaming down his chin.

The next day his son went to live with Delilah and his uncle, Jon, where Cam's altered nature could not betray him, and his uncle's magic could keep him safe.

Cam cursed as the ambushing memory faded. He was better off keeping distant until the gifting day came, until it made no difference what piece Cam held of Anai. He could not be around his son without the risk of betraying Lance's existence. He'd come perilously close already. Heck, he didn't even *think* his son's name for fear some fae might be able to lift it from his thoughts.

That was why he kept separate and did not reveal the true depth of his love. Once he did, it would be impossible to keep the boy away; Cam knew that, he could see the hunger for it in Lance's eyes. They spent time together every once in a while, here or at *Delilah's*, but Cam just didn't understand this magic stuff and the fear his presence would harm his son always sent him running before very long.

Once the boy turned forty-five then they could see how much damage Cam had done. See if hatred had taken root, or if love was stronger. See if it was too late for a father to love his son and be loved back. Would they finally share his Anai at last? And what would that mean for Lance? One week and ten years and they would find out, wouldn't they? Cam could only hope.

Footsteps sounded on the driveway interrupting his tormented thoughts. Cam swore again and slammed the trashed carburetor into the garbage. It had to be Jake; frankly, no one else was brave enough to ignore Cam's barking. But not today. Cam couldn't take it.

"I told you to stop coming around," he growled, heartache mimicking aggression in every line of his body as he spun to confront the kid, this time determined to convince him to stay away.

It wasn't Jake.

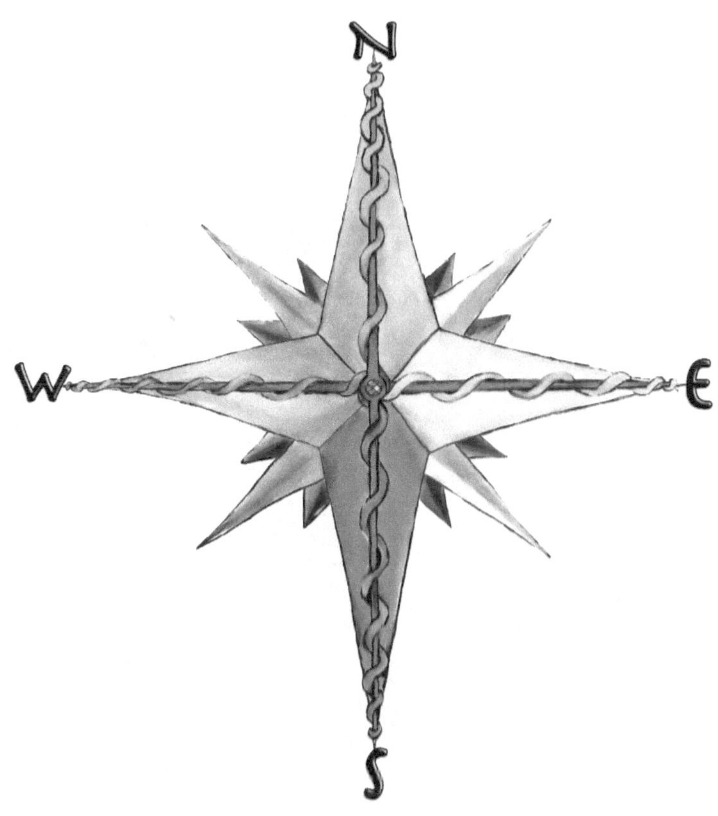
N
W
E
S

Blow and Rock.

Chapter Nine

Lance's mood didn't improve as he ran a circuit of the bar. He couldn't find Jon or Delilah anywhere. The same went for Suzanne, Gavin, and the Winds. In fact, at the moment, mostly locals filled the place, with a couple of lone-wolf bikers playing pool at the back table.

"What's going on, Kelly?" Lance demanded as he stepped up to the counter.

"Couldn't tell ya, Wind Walker," she answered as she tended the bar with a dexterity he had to admire even now, pouring and dressing three different drinks without missing a step, despite his glower. "Mongo might know; he's been here longer than me today."

"Thanks," he grumbled and headed for the kitchen. As the door swung shut behind him Garm lifted his head from the tiles and greeted Lance with a muted woof. He then lay down once more and returned to snoring in record time. Lance shook his head and looked around at Mongo's controlled chaos. He was struck by the sharp contrast it made to Kelly's bartending. Each was a master at what they did but their styles couldn't be more radically different.

"Hey, Mongo," Lance called out. No answer. The cook continued dicing onions with single-minded determination as if he hadn't heard a thing.

"Yo! MONGO!"

Garm gave another muted woof, this time in distinct protest, but Mongo gave no noticeable reaction to either of them. Lance stalked across the kitchen only to have the cook whirl around right before he reached him.

"Outamykitchen!" he snapped, "You know better than to come tramping around here at lunchtime!"

Lance just pinned him with a look that would have melted steel.

"Fine! Quick, then. Whaddaya want?"

"Delilah?"

With more grumbling and a disgusted look Mongo flung his hand toward the kitchen door, the one that led to the compound out back, and returned to his knife and chopping board, slicing and dicing with even more energy than before, not to mention infinitely more grumbling.

Lance slipped out the back door, ignoring him.

He stopped dead on the top step of the stoop. "What the *hell*?!"

The sight before him could have been some demented scene from the Watchmen or something. Everyone he'd been looking for traipsed across the back lot wearing ratty old armor and cheesy grins. They were all, to one degree or another, spattered with great big splotches of neon color. Gavin, Jon, Rock, and Bubba looked ridiculous with soft red hats perched on their heads. They seemed pleased with themselves, though from the looks of things they'd been thoroughly trounced. Rock in particular had barely a clear patch left on him. In contrast, the other team clearly did the trouncing. Dream remained immaculate save for a single pink splotch over her heart and some flecks of spray on the battered old helmet dangling from her hand. Delilah had been tagged only a handful of times. Blow took the worst of it on their side. He looked only slightly less speckled than his brother. And then Lance's gaze landed on Suzanne. She'd pushed back her helmet until it perched on her forehead and definitely walked with a swagger, though she'd been tagged three times, twice at the hip and once on her shoulder. Lance's gaze riveted on a tear in the leather at her other shoulder. It revealed a nasty scratch he meant to ask her about shortly. But for now...damn if she didn't take his breath away. She had a shit-eating grin on her face and a Sheridan pump-action rifle slung over her shoulder. Lance smiled back, his tension running off like sand through his fingers. Moving ahead of the others, Suzanne skipped up the steps as nimble as a doe and just stood before him, grinning.

"Hey, you," he murmured as he took in the glow and her glee. Though he searched her face he could not find any sign of the shadows she'd battled since the crossroads. Oblivious to everything else from the moment his lady had mounted the steps, Lance reached up and tugged the helmet the rest of the way from her head and dangled it from the door knob. He then reached down and slipped the paint gun from her hand. When they were both unencumbered he slid his hands around her hips and settled them on her ass, pulling her snug against him as he took her mouth like a starving man at the feast. She flowed against him, settling her curves hard against his body from neck to knee. Lance heard something in the background, not that he cared; Suzanne, however, laughed and tugged her lips away, her hand smoothing down his shirt where she'd reached beneath it.

His shirt. Lance cursed, then scowled in confusion as he looked down at her hand resting calm against the red fabric. She laughed again and hugged him. "See, I took care of it," she murmured.

Lance's gaze swept over the group again—this time noticing Bubba's family coming up from behind, none of them paint-spattered, and the boys, various paint guns slung over their shoulders, sprawled in a fit of fake gagging—it finally sank in what Suzanne had been up to with the red caps and the trouncing.

"You didn't let the boys play?" Lance asked.

Suzanne gave him a wry grin. "The point was to *improve* my self-confidence, not trample it."

The boys laughed, as did Lance, but he made sure she could see the pride in his eyes. "Aren't you clever?"

She grinned and nodded, clearly pleased with herself. Laughing harder, he couldn't help but caress her rear, still conveniently nestled in the palm of his hand.

"Alright, already!" Sammy called out. "My boys don't need you givin' them ideas!" Her words weren't too heated, though, as the boys were back to the gagging, striving to outdo themselves with melodrama, setting everyone off in another laugh that dispelled the last vestiges of Lance's tension.

That is, until he noticed the slight bulge in Suzanne's front pocket and playfully tugged the item free. "What'ya hiding?" he murmured so only she could hear. He quickly forgot his playful innuendo as he looked down at the scrap of cloth in his hand. Half was moist; the rest was stiff and dry. And brown.

The moist, flexible half was bright crimson.

His gaze jerked up to pin hers in place. "Suzanne?"

The laughter stopped.

Suzanne just stared at him, the grin still on her face, but her eyes solemn and steady. "It's nothing. I took care of it." The last words held a thick ribbon of satisfaction.

Lance nodded and eased back on the testosterone.

"I bet you did, angel." He then glanced from the back door to those waiting on the ground. "Best we go around to the front today, unless Delilah wants to find a new cook before dinner; Blow and Rock are practically dripping and Mongo's on a tear." He slung his arm across Suzanne's shoulder and they started down the stairs. They made it one step down from the top when something slammed into his chest, sending him sprawling backward and then sliding down the rest of the stairs. By some miracle he didn't take Suzanne with him. He saw violent flashes behind his eyes as his head bounced off the concrete, and his chest felt like a SWAT team had taken him out with a battering ram. It took several blinks before he could see. Bad idea. He squeezed his eyes shut again as his attempt to look down for a gaping wound in his chest sent an explosion through his head.

Vaguely, he heard mass panic around him and felt hands looking for damage. Strangely, none of them went toward his chest. He groaned and shoved them away, his own hand going to the point of the most pain. He didn't feel a thing. Of course, he wasn't at his most reasonable at the moment. Rather than risk another detonation, he brought the hand up before his eyes. He'd expected blood, or at best, neon pink paint.

He saw nothing but smooth, clean skin.

Scrambling to his feet he swayed and grabbed for the railing. His head fell back and his body bobbed forward and back in a slight state of shock as he realized he wasn't breathing. It felt like a hand pressed against him, branding his chest, and then a nova blazed beneath his breast bone. He gasped and arched and would have fallen, but for his bulldog-grip on the rail.

And then he experienced something only ephemerally felt before:

His mother's love.

Followed by the nearness of his father's pending death.

"NO!" Lance screamed in anguish. The nova spun around him, making him the center of a whirlpool. He became the convergence for more mage power than he ever conceived, instantly drawn from everything around him though he'd made no effort to summon the energy. His wings flared like the hottest center of a flame and he felt as if his molecules would fly apart. Vaguely he sensed when Dream and Bubba both threw up shields barely in time to protect those around him, but the rest of Lance's focus was locked on the peril surrounding his father. He stared hard at Jon and forced enough breath into his own lungs to growl, "We have to get to Cam's."

And then he vanished in a vortex of mage energy.

He landed on his feet.

Barely.

What the hell!? His powers may have gotten stronger once the fae half dominated but nothing as strong as what had just happened. He hadn't planned to teleport. Didn't even know he could. That was a new trick; one Lance certainly had no clue on how to repeat. Wasn't sure he wanted to, either. He stood in Cam's driveway, legs splayed and his head weaving, trying to get his focus straight. "Shit," he gasped out. Now that he'd forced the issue, his lungs remembered the habit of breathing—but they hadn't gotten down the finer points yet and he found himself heaving like a bellows one moment and gasping the next. It was an effort, but he drew deep, centering breaths, shook the tension from his shoulders, and tried to ignore the persistent warmth burning in his chest, which had almost settled down to nothing more than a toasty ball of energy slowly taking root beside his heart.

And he'd thought he'd been messed up after the encounter with the *Dubh Fae.*

Yeah, Pop, don't worry, the cavalry's arrived...

Enough! he chastised himself, *Get your act together and save the old man, before you lose him too!*

Lance looked up to spy his father in a twisted heap on the ground, a pool of blood gathering on the pavement. Just beyond him the *Dubh Fae* stalked toward them. Fury glittered and sparked in his eyes. "You!" The *Dubh Fae's* wings unfurled with a snap as magic crackled in a nimbus around him. The right wing as tattered as before, the left—the one damaged by Lance's bowie knife the first time they'd fought— barely formed, and still as the *Dubh Fae* flung out his hand Lance knocked back on his heels, but that was all. A cocky grin sliding across his face as the 'Blood band tingled on his finger. "Me," Lance mockingly tossed back at the *Dubh Fae*, as he moved to stand between his father and the fae.

A snarl twisted the *Dubh Fae's* lips as he murmured the words of a spell.

Lance didn't wait. He called upon the surrounding mage energy, picturing a mage bolt, something he had often seen before, though never wielded. The energy moved sluggishly and kept scattering. Lance's head pounded the harder he tried. He gave it up and pulled back before the effort crippled him. Teleporting must have burnt him out a bit. Lance turned to his old faithful: emotion. He gathered up Cam's pain and the fae's frustration, not to mention any strong emotion lingering within a mile radius, and balled them up with his own fear and love and wrath. He lobbed it like an empathic catapult right at the fae's head.

It merely clipped the fae, deflected by an outside emotional thrust moments before impact. His opponent followed the block with a pinpoint thrust of magic and focused will. Sparks flew off the air two feet in front of Lance's face.

Shit! Someone had done some serious adjusting since they'd last met.

Enough of this; they weren't having some kind of tennis match with each man segregated to their own side. Lance stalked forward, measuring his steps precisely until his booted foot came down on the fae's, pinning it in place for an instant, long enough for Lance to throw an uppercut to the *Dubh Fae's* chin, rattling his cage big-time. Teeth clinked, should have shattered, but the fae bobbed his head to the side so that the punch didn't land straight on. Lance dodged a return swing and danced back as the *Dubh Fae*'s momentum carried him forward. He then aimed a kick at the fae's head, anticipating a satisfying thud, only to have his foot grabbed and thrust away. He spun with the force, tumbled, and rolled to his feet, a predatory grin on his face. This might be fun after all; the fae clearly hadn't been in a bar brawl before, but he was no slouch either.

As Lance braced himself to anticipate and evade the next blow, his finger tingled as before. He felt the warmth of magic gathering, but grimaced when he couldn't pinpoint the direction of the attack. With a nervous shift he tried to glance around to spy who might be working in tandem with the fae, but he couldn't sense anyone nearby.

"You through playing games, *halfling*?" Lance said attempting to egg the fae into action as he gathered his own magical response.

The *Dubh Fae* smirked and plucked a dagger literally out of nowhere, simultaneously pulling the earth from beneath Lance's feet. One moment Lance drew in magic, just shy of wings unfurling, then the dagger sank into his shoulder and he found himself contemplating sky. But not for long, in mimicry of Lance's previous one-two attack, the fae dropped an emotional mountain on Lance's head that blinded him with its intensity.

For the second time that day, he stopped breathing.

It all came from the *Dubh Fae*: hatred…rage…frustration… absolute, unfettered fury. None of it came from external sources. Centuries of emotional baggage, nearly half a millennium of unspent wrath, crashed down on Lance in blow after blow. And it wasn't magic, so the 'Blood band remained dormant against the assault.

Lance snarled and fought to get from beneath the barrage, but he found himself powerless in the face of its intensity. It was an emotional nuke and he was the proving ground. Any anger he had felt in his life was like a pouting child in comparison. He groaned and had to fight his own despair. He could well die here, crushed by a trick he himself taught the dog taking him down.

No. Fucking. Way.

Teeth clenched and breath coming hard and fast, Lance fought the paralysis even as the *Dubh Fae* strode past unhurried toward Cameron. *No!* Lance fought harder. *No!* Harder yet.

"No!" he bellowed as best as he was able. The *Dubh Fae* stopped and looked down, an expression on his face that could have been a snarl or a sneer. Lance still couldn't lift his head enough to tell which. "Keep away...from him, you bastard!"

The *Dubh Fae* laughed, not realizing Lance bent all his will upon moving his right leg, curling it back toward his hand. The fae's response only galvanized him, breaking the gravity of the assault. The pant leg edged up as his knee bent, bringing the boot-top in reach of his hand. More rapid breaths, his eyes squeezed shut as he directed all his concentration on pulling the dagger from its sheath.

The fae's gaze landed on the blade and fury flooded his face. He paled, actually trembled, and then snarled again. Calculation followed right behind. He leaned over, contempt molding his features. The *Dubh Fae*'s reaction acted as a final hammer blow, driving Lance down once more. In a swirl of hastily summoned magic the faerie grabbed the dagger and fled.

The *Dubh Fae*'s response had been visceral and the parting blast left Lance reeling. He had a bad feeling about what just transpired. That dagger would be a specter hovering at the corner of his vision for a long time. That hadn't been simple avarice he'd spied in the fae's gaze; his having the dagger could come to no good end. Lance wondered about the significance of the ancient blade. He realized he was going to have to admit to Gort that he might never get it back.

For half a second, he was tired enough to contemplate giving in to the crushing weight on top of him, the other half of the second he mentally kicked himself in the ass. For the first time ever, his father needed him. He better damn well get his ass moving. It was tough, though. Blood trickled from his knife wound and his body felt crushed by the last attack. Lance strained to rise, but only managed another groan.

Across the way, his father raised an answering groan, the sound weak and fading, but surprisingly Cam was still alive.

Lance leveled his considerable will against the emotional mountain on top of him. Instead of dissecting it piece by piece, he shattered it with a stick of mental dynamite shoved right up its ass. The remnant scattered on the wind, harmless over the wilderness surrounding Cam's land.

And still Lance could not move, physically drained and battered by the assault. But he was stubborn as sin, and pissed to boot. He bucked and shifted, ignoring the pain, until he managed to roll over with his chest raised off the ground, propped up by his good arm. Breathing hard and drenched in an icy sweat, Lance hauled himself ten feet across the blacktop to his father's side, nearly blinded by the pain in his shoulder, coupled with a pounding headache from his earlier whack on the head. He collapsed a foot and a half away from his objective, screaming in pain and frustration as the dagger slammed further into his flesh. If he could only get close enough...if he could only touch him. To have come so far only to have to listen for his father's last breath.

Again. No. Fucking. WAY!

Growling and straining, Lance hauled himself another hand's breadth further and flung his good arm forward. He lay there a long moment just breathing, his fingers clenched into his father's shirt until Cam feebly protested. Lance forced his head up and noted that the tension from his grip tugged against a screwdriver sticking from Cam's chest. The pool of blood beneath both of them steadily grew. The *Dubh Fae* hadn't done that. It was too crazy; it never would have occurred to him. Yet Cam was dying. And by all reckoning, he'd done it to himself.

Lance swore, then clenched down on the heartache inspired by the sight, fighting not to project. He took stock of himself and the resources available to him. Physically, he was spent, but he'd recovered somewhat magically. If he calmed himself and got his focus back, he might pull off some healing, as he did with Suzanne weeks ago. It took precious minutes to marshal his concentration. He breathed deep and slow, focusing on his body, the magic swirling within it, and that added bit of warmth he still hadn't figured out. Only when he'd achieved rock-solid calm did he edge his hand forward and grip the handle of the tool. He had only seconds to clear the way and then flood Cam's wound with healing. It would be a race between him and a bleed-out.

He hesitated, his father's life in his hands. On impulse Lance wrapped his thoughts around the warmth in his chest, finding comfort and balance in its gentle pulse. One more deep breath and he yanked.

Cameron screamed and came off the ground, thrusting his chest hard against Lance's hand. Startled, Lance tightened his mental grip on the warmth and frantically pushed his will, his vision of healing out through his hand and into Cam's body. The warmth diminished, but did not disappear as his father arched impossibly further, then gasped and collapsed back to the ground. Only the harsh sound of his steady breath bore testimony to the successful healing.

For a moment, Lance's world went black and silent.

The pain returned first, followed by the mumble of his father's voice.

"You're alive, Lance, you're alive…and you even gave me back my Anai." Cam's voice cracked and his hand shook. The muttering made no sense, but Lance didn't care. Cam had used his name. Awe and love unabashedly filled his father's expression and for once he didn't bother to hide either. Of course, almost dying might have had something to do with that. Neither of them had energy left for emotional repression. For now Cam was stable, but Lance had not managed a complete healing, as he had with Suzanne. He did note that Cam now had his own bundle of warmth nestled in his chest, and Lance had to wonder. Really, he had no choice; it wasn't like he *understood* what just happened.

"You're still alive," Cam murmured again, tears running down his cheeks. He looked and sounded like an old man, but even as Lance watched the signs of age seemed to fade away until Cam was again the youthful man Lance remembered, if a bit more battered.

"Yeah, and so are you, you stupid fuck." There was no heat at all in Lance's words, only warmth. "Cut it out, I'm not even close to dying. Unlike some of us! Why did you do such a stupid thing?"

"Um…." Cam struggled to focus, weak and still wounded. "Um, I had to stop him. He was gonna take me, use me…um…

against you. Figured a body'd just piss you off, not get you killed."

"Yeah...and the unedited version?"

"I tried to make a run for the house and I fell."

"I can't believe you," Lance muttered his chest tightening at how close he'd come to losing his father. Then he made himself keep talking. His words meant nothing. They were not so important as long as they kept Cameron coherent. He began to babble, none too steady himself. "I can't tell you how many times you told me to respect the damn tools. You call this respect? You're sour old blood's gonna eat the finish right off of that screwdriver. Then what's it worth when corrosion sets in? Huh?" He somehow managed to keep his voice from cracking.

Cam choked on a laugh and Lance's breath caught, this time in his throat, as he silently cursed himself.

He dragged himself closer, determined to hug his father one more time, and best do it now, when he couldn't flinch away, instead of trying later when he might evade the effort. He only managed an arm across Cam's chest, but he gently squeezed, despite his own agony. As he shifted his head to the side he caught sight of what was left of the Knucklehead beside them.

"Hey," Lance said, as they lay spent in the sun, waiting for someone to come scrape them up. "You started without me!" He tried not to think of the knife lodged in his shoulder or the way his body throbbed and ached along every inch. Breathing was still something he had to concentrate on doing.

His old man managed fine, though, his strength returning much quicker than Lance's. He brought his arm up and around in his own hug, unaware of the agony he caused as he unknowingly jostled the *Dubh Fae*'s blade. Lance gladly bore the pain. "Oh, come on, it's not like you ever had any patience for the tear-down. You were always too anxious for the build to appreciate it."

Lance heard depth in Cameron's voice that had been missing for most of his life. Lance liked it, despite the exasperation mixed in. "Oh, like any ham-fisted poser can't take something apart; it takes skill to put together a sweet ride."

"Maybe, but can any poser take something apart so's you can still use the bits after?"

Feeling the overwhelming need to make sure the other still breathed—at least on Lance's part—they continued to snipe at one another until the rumble of cycles sounded in the distance drawing near. They fell silent and gently eased away from one another only as the first bike roared into the driveway, swerving into the garbage cans in an effort not to plow into them.

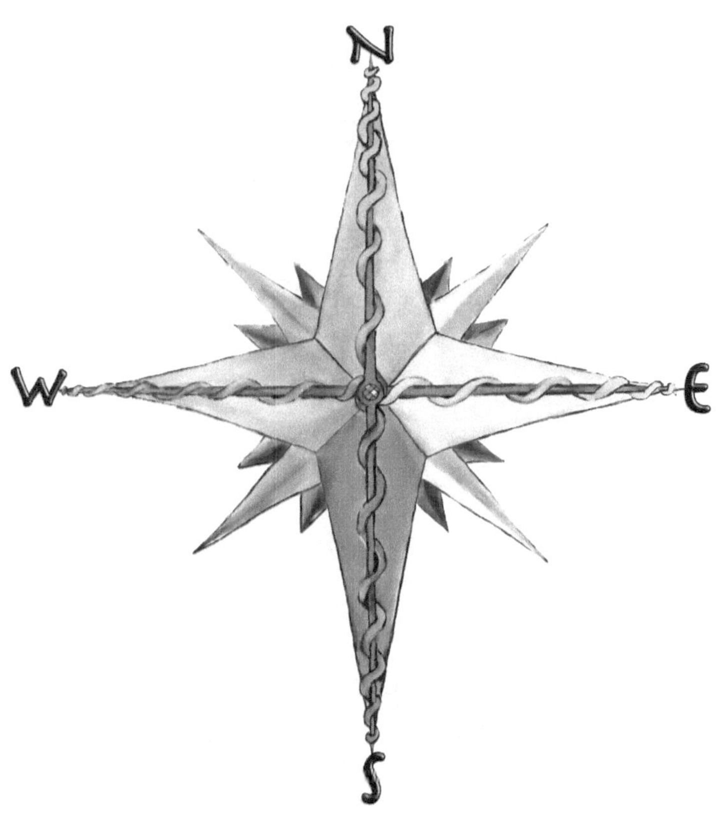

N
W
E
S

Garm

Chapter Ten

CAMERON COSAIN WAS A STUBBORN MAN. SO WAS HIS SON.

They stood in that driveway and argued for ten minutes solid because Cam insisted on staying where he was. The Four Winds and Gavin stood several feet away beside their bikes trying to pretend they weren't impatient and that they couldn't hear every word.

"You nearly died!"

"Yeah," Cam said and his lips pursed as he looked down at the hole in his favorite shirt. "But you took care of that. Now go on, I'll be fine right here; besides, I got to finish this break-down." A twinkle lit his father's eyes that any other time would have made Lance the happiest man in the world. Right now it drove him nuts.

"You're shields didn't work, old man!"

Cam nodded but sat down firmly in his chair, which he'd flipped around to face the end of the drive. "Maybe, but I figure that's because he was a halfling and not all fue, an' I wasn't payin' attention. Don't figure they have too many halflings can do what he did. And they certainly won't sneak up on me again." He calmly patted the shotgun he'd placed beside the chair. Lance opened his mouth to protest again and Cam cut him off. "Boy, go home, get yourself patched up the rest of the way before it's you I'm buryin', then get your ass back over here soon and pull your weight on this rebuild. Don't go thinkin' I'm gonna do it all for you."

Now, that was a bit of exaggeration. Gavin had done a rough patch job on his shoulder, so Lance wasn't in any immediate danger. He tried to snipe back but his vision greyed out and his body swayed.

"Whoa!" Cameron reached out an arm to steady him as the others rushed forward ready to catch. But it wasn't necessary. Something odd happened. Something fae.

The kernels of warmth in each of their chests flared and for a moment Lance had the sensation the separate balls of energy became one again. He grunted, as did Cam, and this time both swayed slightly before their stance steadied.

Lance suspected he looked just as stunned as his father did. Each of them felt the wound in Lance's shoulder flow together and seal as his father wished him well. Cam had no magic, not even empathy, but apparently whatever Lance's mother had gifted them with allowed him to heal his son.

Their eyes met and Lance nodded. Respecting Cam's choice he gripped his father's shoulder and turned to head for the bikes. "Catch you later, Dad. Have to go kick some faerie ass."

Cameron laughed behind him as Lance swung onto the back of Bubba's Fat Boy and the members of the Wild Hunt sped away.

They weren't far from *Delilah's*, maybe ten miles away. They'd barely opened the throttle before they pulled into the lot and swung off their bikes. Their brows dipped as the seven of them glanced around at the packed lot. *Delilah's* was popular, and most of the Hunt had made it into town in response to the summons, but it didn't feel right that they'd all converged so soon before the meeting time.

"Something's wrong," Lance murmured. For once he rode pillion, leaving him nothing to do as the others locked down their cycles. He spun on his heel and headed inside. Before he even opened the door, he heard the uproar inside. "Guys, something is *wrong*," he called over his shoulder, raising his voice a bit louder as he pushed into the bar. The others abandoned their bikes as-is and followed.

The first thing Lance saw was Suzanne perched on top of the bar. The second was Delilah pacing in front of it. He barely recognized his aunt. Her normally neat hair whipped about her as she went from one end of the bar to the other, her eyes—tinged a bit mad and a lot dangerous—darted from the door to the faces of those forming a wall between her and the way out. Lance noticed no few of them bore minor wounds: scratches and bites and not a few black eyes. Mongo stood alone, unscathed, blocking the kitchen door. Every few paces Delilah growled at everyone, ferocity billowing from her like smoke from a California wildfire. Her eyes flared brightly as Lance and those with him came through the front door. She launched herself at the human barricade the moment she met his eye; the bikers wisely fell away, their job done.

"She's gone!" Delilah screamed. No one needed ask who. There was an innate rage peculiar only to mothers. "She's gone! They *took* her and you *will* get her back!" She punctuated the words with her hard little fist, pounding it into Lance's healed, but tender shoulder. He jerked back and brought his hands up to still her.

"Yes." That was all he said, quiet and lethal.

It was like someone punched a hole in her gas tank. She stilled, then trembled, then her legs gave out as a single sob broke loose. Lance drew her close before she fell but she wasn't in his grip for more than thirty seconds before Jon pulled her away into the shelter of his arms.

"Dair na Scath?"

Jon nodded, murder in his gaze. "He sent his knight, Callan, through a temporary gate anchored to Gort's face."

"What?!"

"The wound contained a splinter of oak, enough to allow Dair to bypass the protections. The bells didn't even ring. We wouldn't have known at all if Gort hadn't fallen down the stairs trying to get help."

Lance cursed. "Where is he?"

His uncle just looked at him kind of lost, caught in the grip of grief and self-recrimination as Delilah cried quietly into his shirt. Lance shook his head and gripped Jon's shoulder, pushing him and Delilah to a booth in the corner where they could have some quiet to get themselves together. His uncle's murmurs as they moved off fed the wrath kindling in Lance's chest. He stalked forward to the center of the bar, stance wide and his muscles taut; adrenaline washed away the last of his aches as he turned in a circle, meeting the gaze of each biker crammed into the bar. He stopped turning when he spied Gort slumped in the corner with Garm at his feet. The fae stared out into space, his hand moving over the dog's coat as if of its own volition. Lance stalked over and hauled Gort up by the collar of his shirt, shook him hard until the fae's eyes returned to focus, then he let go.

"Back room, *now.*"

By the time Gort stumbled in—looking like someone had tried to turn him into Garm's dinner—Lance closed the door on the heels of the last biker. Slow and silent, he turned and locked gazes with Gort.

"I swear to you, I was no conscious part of this." Gort's words came out a bit mushed compared to his normal crispness, but Lance understood what he said…in more ways than one.

He didn't respond, though. In silence he considered the fae. Bruises mottled his face and one side of his mouth was swollen and misshapen. A slash on his left arm spoke of more than fists brought to bear, and the way he stood slightly hunched on that side made Lance wonder if a few ribs weren't broken as well. What caught his eye, though, was the wound Gort had arrived with: It had torn open from the inside and something left a wide gouge. None of the wounds had been treated and the worst still bled, but the majority of them already began to heal on their own, which made Lance wonder how bad they'd been to begin with.

"Are you done?" Gort demanded with tattered dignity. "Or do you wish to add to my torment? I assure you, short of killing me, you couldn't make me feel worse."

Lance cocked his head and took a deep breath to steady himself. His emotional control wasn't so good at the moment. He had to throttle down on the impulse to add to Gort's wounds. Before Lance could trust himself to respond, the muscles in Gort's battered face twitched and jumped as if he resisted defending himself further. A few more moments of silence and he huffed out a breath, his expression settled into a glower. "I tried!"

Lance nodded slow and steady. "I know. If my gang did this you wouldn't be standing, so you must have already convinced someone. Frankly, I don't care."

Gort's brow twisted with confusion as Lance failed to live up to his expectations. The fae swore and slumped into the nearest chair as if standing any longer was beyond him. "What do you want?"

"I want my cousin back. I want her safe and sound and in her mother's arms before Delilah maims somebody. And I want Dair to back the hell off and keep to his own side of the Veil the way we stick to ours. Got it?"

Gort nodded, but did not speak, his expression bleak and resigned.

"You were trusted with something precious and you fucked up. Make it right," Lance said, then headed for the door.

"Wait...please...." Gort called out, his voice thin, tired.

Lance stopped and looked over his shoulder. "Go on."

"I was given...a message for you."

No surprise there. Pivoting, Lance turned around and crossed his arms over his chest. He tilted his chin upward and narrowed his eyes.

Gort just sighed and lowered his head, his expression pained and his tone flat. "Meet him alone at the field of Destiny, with the dagger—the one you took from me—and he will allow you to exchange yourself for the woman."

Lance actually laughed, startling the fae. "Do I *look* stupid? Or just *human*?" He shook his head and settled in the chair across from Gort. "I go to this field and I'm on faerie soil. Even if I trusted him to keep his word, even if I were willing to roll over and take this instead of kicking his ass, there is no way in hell I'd do it alone, on his turf, with no one to see she makes it home."

That made Gort both smile and wince. "Not stupid, wise."

Then Lance grimaced. "There's another problem."

Gort looked up and gave a little tilt to his head, clearly waiting for Lance to go on. Lance didn't want to. He'd known when it had happened this would come back to bite him in the ass; well now, he was about to find out how hard.

"What problem?" Gort prompted him.

The room felt close and hot again, as it had the night before. Lance shifted in his chair and glanced up from beneath this brow, before bringing his fisted hand down on the table. "I don't have it anymore."

Gort came to his feet, knocking the chair half across the room.

"What?! What do you mean you no longer have it?"

It was the loudest Lance had ever heard the fae speak. The door flew open in response to the commotion. Waving off those that poked their heads in the door, Lance sat forward and waited until it closed again.

"It was taken from me by the *Dubh Fae*, when he was trying to kill me."

Gort groaned and turned away, muttering, his body stiff with tension and his steps forceful as he paced. "You have no idea...*great goddess*, you have no idea...."

Yeah. Lance felt a big ole bite coming on.

"So why don't you tell me already," he snapped.

"Dipped in the mingled blood of the *Rudha-an* line and the one to be king, the dagger's magic binds them to the throne. One can sit the throne without the ritual, but both monarch and land are then diminished. Dair needs it to bind his rule...Kerwin...the *Dubh Fae*...needs it to steal the throne."

"Tils...Tilly is of the *Rudha-an* line...as are you. If they can gain control of one of you and the dagger they will have all they need to revive the magic of Underhill and the *Rudha-an* rule, all of it at the control of the victor."

Lance cursed and pushed to his own feet, his hand raking through his hair and his gut going sour. "Yeah, sorry to disappoint either one, but that is not happening. We don't have time to track the *Dubh Fae* down. Can we fake the blade, just long enough to get our hands on Tilly?"

Gort stopped pacing and looked over his shoulder at Lance. "We can try to instill some mage energy into another blade, then wrap it to mask the fact that it is not the true dagger. It may work, but it will not last long."

"It only has to get us into the party," Lance said. "How do I get a message to the *Ard Ri*?"

"Move beyond your shields, to the nearest oak," the fae said. "Whisper among its branches what you would have him hear. If the leaves fold up, he agrees. If they fall off...he does not,"—Gort reached a hand to his damaged cheek—"in which case, I advise returning to protected ground with all due haste."

The chair squealed as Lance pushed to his feet.

"Where would he consider neutral?"

"Avalon."

"Excuse me?!" Lance shook his head, wondering which was more responsible for Gort's scrambled brains: watching TV, or being repeatedly pummeled in the head. "As in, the resting place of King Arthur?"

"Not all elements of legend are false."

"Yeah? Well, I don't exactly have the time or the means to head to England for this."

"They call you Wind Walker?" Gort asked, his eyes gleaming, what could be seen of them. He seemingly ignored Lance's comment.

Lance nodded cautiously.

"That is a good name to have in this." The fae sat forward and his voice dropped down. "In these exact words, tell the *Ard Ri* you exercise your right of challenge, that you will meet him at Avalon above with dagger in hand and naught but the *four winds* to witness."

Now that brought an appreciative smile to Lance's face. "Sneaky bastard...knew I liked you."

This time Gort laughed, winced once again, and then shook his head. "No, you don't."

"Hmmm...maybe, maybe not," Lance answered as he turned to leave. "You can get us there?"

Gort nodded.

He paused by the door, "Have Jon clean you up again, and tell him to get you ready to ride."

The leaves did not fall off the tree, though Lance did feel the sharp sting of a few slung acorns as he turned away. Gort hadn't said anything about acorns. Lance flipped off the tree over his shoulder; it felt appropriate to respond in kind. Then he returned to the bar and had Kelly ring the meeting bell. Again.

"Enough is enough." They all fell silent as he addressed the club. "We didn't take crap from the Red Dawgs, or even the Raptors, who were a much more serious threat to our turf.

"We're not taking it from Dair na Scath and his faerie Court, either. Thanks to some fancy wording, the Winds will be with me. No one else, but I want the Hunt nearby, ready to kick some faerie ass if they try and pull a fast one. Patch holders gear up, break out your toys if you have them." In short order, the fae visibly bristled with blades of all sizes, the humans bore a good number of knifes and lengths of pipe, plus a few chains slung across shoulders. No guns—they didn't allow them in the bar because of Tilly. She had a thing for guns from before her accident. Had even been a recognized marksman on the range. Before. Now she was a danger to more than herself with a pistol in her grip. Fortunately, this crew didn't need them.

He started calling out names, dividing the masses into two groups: one to stay behind to protect the families, the other to ride the Wild Hunt against the fae. Except for his toughest brawlers, the humans stayed behind, better able to serve at *Delilah's* where the shields on the place evened the field when it came to magic. Likewise, most of the fae and halflings got tagged for the rescue run, except for Jon (who was needed to anchor Delilah), Suzanne, and one or two others to provide a magical arsenal for those left behind.

None of those chosen to guard were pleased, but Lance cut them off with a glance before they could argue. "Stay here and do your part, or turn in your colors."

And he meant it. Even for Suzanne. She knew it too. Her jaw hardened and her eyes went cold as her fingers twitched. "I can handle this," she growled.

Lance nodded and shored up his resolve, not about to give in, even if it meant she turned from him. "Good, glad to hear it, but I still need you to *handle* it here." He was bald-faced honest with her. "You are my strongest mage, and my biggest distraction. I need you to stay here to protect the families not because I don't think you're up to the battle, but because I can't afford to not have my head in the fight."

He held his breath as her temper flared and her hand inched closer to the colors. "I'm trusting you, angel...I'm trusting you with your life, with theirs, I'm just not ready for you to be in harm's way, not against these kind of odds. I need to know you're safe. You only just kicked this and I'm already rattled. Right now, *I* can't handle it." He pled with her silently as he couldn't afford to do aloud. She didn't look happy, but some of the heat in her gaze banked back and she nodded sharply as she turned and stomped away, disappearing through the door to the back room.

Inside Lance turned to stone. He feared he'd just done serious damage to their relationship, but even so, he couldn't have played it any other way. Steeling himself, he turned and waved his riders out the door. The others followed behind them as if there was something they might miss in the parking lot.

Those heading out mounted up to the fierce rallying cry of those staying behind. Lance headed for his father's Panhead with Gort following close. The fae looked the part, decked out in a spare set of Gavin's leathers, but his eyes held wariness as he stopped beside the cycle; his grip white-knuckled around the decoy blade. Lance ignored Gort's tension the best he could and ran a quick visual check on the cycle, when Suzanne stalked out of the bar and thrust a huge box at him. Once her hands were free she dropped one of the bells from the Guardian wall on top.

"Happy Birthday." Between her clenched jaw and her lethal scowl, Lance had to laugh. She certainly looked like she wished him very happy at the moment...*not.* Still, she couldn't be too pissed to have brought this to him now. His birthday was a week away and it wasn't exactly the time for gifts. Whatever the box held must be something she figured would increase his chances of coming home in one piece, and under his own steam. He pulled off the lid and tossed it aside revealing a brand-new set of armor. He whistled as he fingered the thick, supple leather, noted briefly the runes running down the length from neck to cuff, a peculiar mix of ogham runes and fae script that sang to his senses with their latent power. Across the back, of course, was the Wild Hunt logo, and beneath that the name the Winds had given him: Dušan. *Spirit.* Oddly, there were no slits for his wings, which brought a bit of a frown to his face. He quickly smoothed it away, but Sue must have caught it.

"It's not an issue," she said cryptically as he ran his hand over the back. He nodded and gave her a grin.

Too bad he hadn't had this set of armor when he'd encountered Smear or the Dubh Fae. Things might have rolled out different. Lance wasted no time stripping down right there and slipping them on like a second skin. His thunderbolt went into his hip pocket and his bowie knife into a clever sheath built into the pant leg along the calf. Straightening, he turned to thank Suzanne properly and she instead shoved a new, high-end helmet at him—shield spelled like the one he'd lost, from the feel of it—then stalked away before he could say a thing. That didn't surprise him; after all she was understandably pissed. He was floored, however, as he heard her mutter "love you" under her breath. The first time she ever said the words.

"I love you too," he murmured back, knowing she could hear him. She didn't break stride but her tat noticeably hugged his arm tighter at his words. With a whoop, Lance spun, a wild grin on his face as he straddled the cycle. He and Gort were the last to mount up. It was weird having a guy on the pillion pad, but Lance needed his intel source close at hand.

"Let's ride!" he yelled and a jumble of Celtic cries, war whoops, and revving engines answered. Lance took Front Door and opened the throttle full.

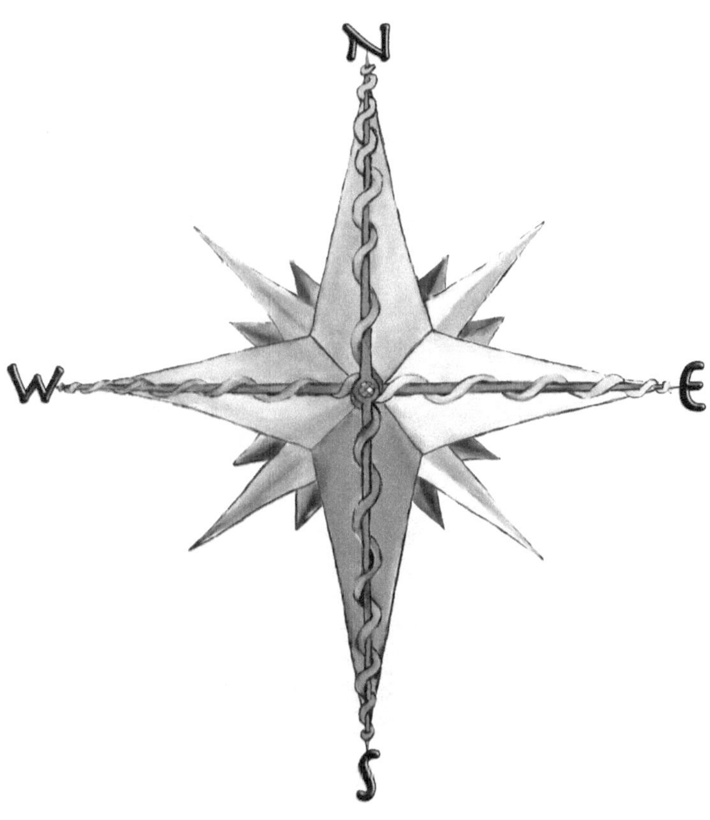

N
W
E
S

Callan

Chapter Eleven

Underhill reflected the demeanor of its King. The dark and the dangerous crept out of the gloaming as a world-ending storm roiled overhead. Fae creatures screamed and the land itself grew ugly as it reflected Dair na Scath's madness and echoed his fury. Thunder sounded overhead, echoed by his mount's hooves. The trees clattered a furious uproar as the fae army passed. Callan rode beside him, restraining the halfling. The vicious little beast had started to come around, thrashing mightily even against the strength of his greatest warrior. She screamed and snapped her teeth with impotent rage, though her eyes were not more than half open. She was responsible in no small measure for the tempest overhead. Dair's hand went to the claw marks at his throat; his other hand, where it rest against his aching thigh, clenched.

Were she not of *Rudha-an* blood she'd already be dead.

"Put the sleep to her before we forget either of you serves a purpose," Dair growled.

Callan dutifully drew upon his power and—with his expression twisted in distaste—laid his lips upon the halfling's head. Dair felt the struggle and, though the matter was an annoyance, part of him thrilled at her strength that his mightiest fae required such effort to subdue her. The girl had been taken as a weapon against the Abomination, but upon seeing her, Dair knew she would be so much more; halfling though she be herself, and flawed in her reasoning, she was of Rowan blood and the last female of that line. She would be enough—once he had the dagger back—to bind him fast to the throne he held so tightly for all time. And being Jonraphal's get, she was no blood of his. Dair would bind her mind and wed her true, unlike Anaiphal, his faithless daughter, who wed him in name, and fled before the binding.

He cursed Gort, the vilest of betrayers, for stealing away the dagger, or the deed would already be done. It occurred to Dair that it was unwise to let her from his side, until after the binding. "Pass her to me," he ordered his warrior. "I will need you unencumbered."

Silently, the knight complied.

As they crossed through the gate away from the fae lands, Dair latched onto a piece of its glamour, held it tight as he rode forward until it stretched out behind him like a canopy above his forces. When the last crossed the threshold, Dair released his grip and willed the glamour down until all but he were enshrouded. In silence, they marched across the mundane countryside, weirding weather left behind, but not the rage from which it had spawned.

Summoning power to his hand, Dair na Scath drew down the clouds to carry his veiled forces to the shores of Avalon.

The Wild Hunt roared over country road to dirt track to wilderness path, Lance guided by Gort's seemingly disembodied hand reaching past his ear. The ride didn't take long; Gort led them to a meadow about a quarter mile behind Cam's house, part of a campground that had closed years ago. From the number of lesser fae Lance sensed among the trees he could imagine why. Dismounting, he waved Gavin over for some last-minute instructions.

"We aren't alone here, so don't get too comfortable," Lance told him, nodding toward the tree line and scanning the tall grasses, which rippled and danced, though there was little wind. "You're in charge, so don't let anyone pull rank. They don't know what they're facing here, even those that have had some dealing with the fae. Either they listen to you, or they deal with me later. Make sure they understand. They don't want to deal with me."

Gavin gave a half grin at that.

"You see our colors in the sky," Lance told Gavin, "come join the fun, got it?" Gavin nodded. "If this goes to all shit—you head back to *Delilah's*...and keep them safe." His lieutenant's expression went grim as he nodded again, then turned away to join the rest of the club setting up a very rough camp in the clearing.

Lance pushed his cycle among the others and lowered the kick stand. He then turned to where the Winds waited, their bikes already stowed. He noticed Sammy standing beside the South Wind, her chin jutting and her hands fisted on her hips. Sammy, who hadn't been tagged to come, who had two boys that would be left alone in the world if neither parent came home.

"Not happy about this, Nur," Lance growled, using the South Wind's chosen name. The cusp of battle did not seem the time for legals.

"Yeah," Nur spat back. "Like I am! Sammy goes where she damn well pleases, she doesn't need me to get around. Short of sinking her into four feet of rock I couldn't keep her from comin', and I'm not worried enough about her to piss her off that much."

Lance couldn't help the grim laugh that forced from him. It was easy to forget the pixie had mojo of her own. Her gaze burned fiercer than her husband's, though her eyes held no actual flame. Wing-shaped shimmers arched at her back where the glamour thinned; she must have been really revved up for that to happen. He didn't know why, but she never showed her wings. If Lance looked closely he could see the serrated edges of her teeth just past her rosy lips. He made it a point not to. Then Nur's words registered.

Lance stepped up and got into the pixie's face.

"You can't go up with us, Samandrea," Lance told her, his tone steely. "Do you understand? You can't put one *foot* onto Avalon, or we'll never get Tilly out of there.

"I'm already playing fast and loose here bringing the Winds. Politics suck, but if they keep this civil and the *Ard Ri* in line, we've got to play them. *We* can't be the ones to violate neutrality."

Sammy scowled at him.

"Understood?" Lance stared her hard in the eye until she gave a jerking nod. He did not, however, miss the glimmer in her gaze. He prayed she did not miss the one in his. He turned and walked out into the field, standing knee deep in the lush meadow grass. "What now?" he asked as he watched dusk settle.

Gort stood from where he'd quietly perched on the seat of the Panhead. "You must petition one of the nine that rule Avalon. Each of you ascending must draw to you your power and make known your wish to enter their realm."

Anatu cocked her hip and planted a fist on it. "What are the rules, faerie man?"

"Only those agreed upon may go, weapons are not banned, but hostilities are prohibited." Gort answered, ignoring the insult. "Nothing more, save what is dictated by common courtesy."

Enlil stepped up beside his half-brother, a mock-sorrowful look upon his face. "Sorry, man, looks like you'll have to stay here." Enki growled and shoved him back with a less-than-gentle nudge of his elbow.

Lance ignored their sniping and turned to Gort. "What happens if someone doesn't play nice?"

"The ladies of Avalon deal with them as they deem appropriate."

"Good to know," Lance said as he eyed the brothers. "Okay, let's get this done. Who has the dagger?"

Enki held up the prepared bundle. It was Jon's Court dagger, the one he'd carried into exile, already steeped in magic and similar enough to the true blade to pass at first glance.

The Winds each moved instinctually to their cardinal points, centered on Lance. He shook the tension from his shoulders and took a deep breath. He was about to gather in the ambient energy surrounding the meadow when a woman's tetchy voice spoke into his thoughts, *"Oh, come on already!"*

With no more ceremony than that, the five bikers disappeared from the meadow, leaving Gort staring at nothing but tall grasses thrashing in the twilight and the flicker of fireflies beneath the trees.

They landed on a beach of soft blue sand the subtle and varied shades of a spring sky. Behind them rose a graceful fortress, brilliantly white and of no determinable architectural period. Three wide, low-rising steps led to an open archway, but there was no one in sight. The building overlooked an ocean of clouds lapping the shore.

Dair waited for them there among the billows, mounted on a steed that bore little resemblance to a horse beyond possessing four legs. It gave the impression of being made from coral, only the living organism, not the bleached and hardened remains found washed up on the beach. The head on its long, thick neck resembled something like a moray eel's—complete with needle-like teeth. The feet were vaguely hoof-like...if the hoofs were split, wedge-shaped blades riding half up what would be the fetlocks on a more usual mount. Tilly rode double behind the High King, her expression even more muddled than usual and her face stark white with anxiety.

"They were not to be here, halfling." Dair's tone was cold and furious as he swept his gaze over Lance's companions.

Lance held his breath, waiting for the ladies of Avalon to sound in judgment. But silence ruled it a righteous call. The Four Winds had been duly, if slyly, declared and thus they stayed.

Sorry to inconvenience you, Lance thought sarcastically at the *Ard Ri* as he let satisfaction show in his expression just to piss Dair off. The woman's voice chuckled in his head, somewhat less tetchy than previously. He ignored both her and Dair.

"Tilly, honey, get down from there," Lance called to his cousin, figuring it was worth a try.

Dair smirked. "*Tilsaia,* remain where you are. And settle." Dair's voice sounded as smooth and soft as low-nap velvet. There was something in the words or the way they were said, something that calmed Tilly like a cat coming down off a catnip high. Her eyes glazed further and her head came to rest on Dair's shoulder. Ten points to the faerie king, because that just pissed Lance off. And Dair used that name, the one Gort had gone on about earlier. It was like they were talking about two different Tillys and all Lance knew is he wanted *his* back.

He growled and stalked forward, whipping out his thunderbolt and flicking it open, ready to see if fresh coral cracked or crumbled. He just barely restrained himself as the air actually tensed around him.

"Don't fuck with me, old man. I've had a bad day."

"Believe us when we tell you, you are the last we'd think to 'fuck' with," Dair answered. "And also believe that we have waited long enough for what is ours. We want the dagger.

"Return it to us,"—again that smoothness—"and we can discuss Tilsaia's disposition."

Lance wished he knew the trick; something subtle tugged at him, urging him to give in, encouraging him to go—of all things—mellow. And not just him, but those at his back as well. He felt them resist, but on the back of the coral beast Tilly nearly fell asleep. Lance steeled himself against the effect and responded.

"Yeah, one problem with that...your goon, the *Dubh Fae*, stole it." Crap! Lance had not meant to reveal that, and yet it seemed he did not have a choice. Apparently lying violated common courtesy...go figure. He couldn't let it throw him, though. Lance unleashed his attitude. "Get a clue, asshole, we're not leaving here without Tilly. Now back off on your mojo before I feed you your nuts."

As he spoke Lance drew in enough power to set his skin tingling, but not enough to flood his wings. Guiding the power with his considerable will, he focused on his cousin, visualizing her mind clear of the cloud subduing her, visualizing the connection between her and the *Ard Ri* severed. It resisted and Lance pushed harder until his own brain screamed.

He sensed the recoil as the siren song affecting her shattered with an audible snap.

Dair recoiled as if physically struck, while behind him Tilly went rigid, and her eyes wide. Lance saw her tremble as she freaked to find herself mounted two-up. That was the one thing that had stuck with her from the accident. She never rode double, except with a few highly trusted members of the Hunt. Shrieking, she shoved hard at Dair's shoulders. The force pushed her back and him forward until each of them fell off their respective ends. Dair's steed went mad, as if it too had been controlled against its will. It whirled and lunged and snapped with its barracuda teeth indiscriminately. With a shrill cry it pivoted away and fled to the shore as Dair surged to his feet, screaming with rage as he drew in masses of power. His wings snapped and lashed about him, phasing in shades of electric blue and green. Tilly cringed away as a tendril licked at her arm with a sizzle. Abruptly the cloudbank behind the *Ard Ri* shimmered, then flashed, revealing the fae host. At their forefront stood an elfin lord Lance presumed to be Callan, the soon-to-be-dead knight.

Shit! So much for neutrality! "Tilly...Dumplin', run to me!" Lance hollered, but Dair blocked her way. Unless Lance did something. Quick and dirty, he reached out and grabbed every bit of magic he could. In an instant he understood what Suzanne had said earlier about the missing slits in his jacket not mattering. He actually felt the cells of the leather slide out of the way to allow his fins to unfurl. Then his wings lashed the air with crackling energy. Huge and opalescent white, they swirled about him like some '70s disco art.

A furious cry sounded to his left as something whizzed by. Lance spun and readied an attack, mentally shaping a spear of light the same way he'd first formed the clapper in the gremlin bell just days ago. He drew back his arm but did not loose the weapon as he caught a glimpse of Sammy's bright red pigtails and upturned nose over a fierce snarl. Thank God, she had understood. The pixie had taken wing and now dove for Tilly, who'd scrambled to her feet, dodging Dair's grasp.

"Damn!" Lance said as he saw Sammy for the first time without her glamour. She had wings like a bat, only graceful, lovely, in cardinal red with patterns swirling like bird's-eye maple. They were stunning, not just in their beauty, but for the wide slashes of blackened scar marking them from finger joint to now-ragged edge. Clearly she could fly, and damn well at that, but the damage had to be painful in more ways than one.

As Sammy drew near, Dair met her attack with a mage bolt, sending her into a screaming spin. The air heated with a sulfurous stink and at Lance's back an answering battle cry rose from four throats, fierce enough to shame a full regiment. Sammy corrected her flight as Nur and Enlil combined efforts to send her a helpful thermal. The others tried to come around to circle them from all sides, but Dair kept shifting, foiling their efforts. In the meantime, Sammy arced back around to circle above Tilly, muttering furiously as Dair kept her at bay. She continued trying to rescue her halfling friend until her strength gave out, forcing Sammy to wing away, back to the meadow below to wait with the rest of the Hunt.

"Dumplin', get your butt over here," Lance called out to Tilly, giving his cousin a focus.

She tried valiantly, her eyes clear and her expression determined, but Dair lunged, grabbing her as she came too close. They disappeared into the ether until all that remained was Lance's temper and the ghost of Tilly's cry.

Then Dair's voice sounded in the air around them, echoing as if in a great empty hall, "The dagger, halfling. Bring me the dagger."

Stunned silence reigned as Lance and the Winds waited for the fae army to attack. The elementals flanked him, North and East to one side, South and West to the other, their chosen weapons to hand, but not raised. Lance, however, was in the mood for Armageddon. He drew in more magic, restoring what he'd used, then added to it until his wings dwarfed even Nur. An image formed in his mind: a rain of daggers, glittering and deadly as they pelted Callan and the rest of Dair's forces and stole away their immortality. It was not a happy thought, but it held some satisfaction. If they were going to take him out, he would bring as many as he could along for company. Lance let the urge to strike build. No longer prepared to wait, to react, he wanted to wreak retribution all over their asses. Now.

The army merely stared back, weapons raise at the ready. They made no other move. The air weighed heavy with a sense of waiting, like a bowstring held taut...or a ship balanced on the verge of sinking.

Lance had enough waiting.

"Stand down, Wind Walker."

That tetchy woman's voice again. Only this time not in his head. Lance growled over his shoulder.

"You would violate neutral ground?"

"What?" He whirled and stalked to the broad steps. They were no longer empty. Nine women stood three to a step, their judging gazes trained on him. "I would violate neutrality? Are you blind? What just happened here!? Let me tell you, your neutrality has already gone to shit!"

Anatu stepped around Lance's wings and came up close in front of him, breaking his line of sight on the ladies. She tapped him upside the head war-goddess style. "Dušan, break it off. You're not seeing it straight. You need to stand down." Lance snarled and would have argued, only Nur made a noise behind him. Nur never called him out. Snapping the tension out of his neck, Lance glanced from the army to the Winds, and back to the ladies once again. Slowly, carefully, he dumped the magic harmlessly back into the air.

"Explain."

Lance felt Nur reach out and gently tug him around by his shoulder. "Look," the South Wind pointed in the direction of Dair's warriors. "What do you see?"

Scowling, Lance considered. The fae army stood in formation, poised to engage, the knight, Callan, at the forefront, a hungry expression narrowing his eyes. The clouds billowed and swirled about their feet leaving no ground visible. Enlil then stepped up to Lance's other side and gripped that shoulder. As he gave it a little squeeze he puffed out a breath with some elemental magic juicing it up. The clouds bobbed on the breeze, drifting slightly until they moved a few feet off from the shore. Dair's army shifted nervously, but held ranks. The wind elemental drew a deeper breath and blew a little harder, until the enemy forces drifted away. Callan stood rigid at the edge, as if he might have leapt across to the shore and engaged the battle, if only reason had not stilled him. They swiftly disappeared from sight.

Grinding his teeth, Lance cursed. He wasn't the only one to play semantics: Dair had not violated the neutrality of Avalon because he'd never set foot *on* Avalon.

Lance turned back to the ladies and bowed his head to them. "I apologize for being discourteous." Delilah would have been proud.

The ladies...they laughed. Lance stilled at that, but kept his reaction under tight rein.

One of the women stepped forward, a tall, tough broad moving much like Anatu did: relaxed and strutting, but with a threat of potential stomping in each step. Her hair was black and short and her eyes the dark grey of gun smoke. On her bared shoulder there was a tattoo of a crow in flight. Lance knew enough of Arthurian legend to figure out this was the Morrigan. She bowed in kind as she came before him, though not so deeply. "You, Wind Walker, may ask us one boon, Dair's forfeit for his deceit; your reward for being clever enough to recognize the game."

Yeah. Real clever, Lance thought. *So clever they had to all but hit me over the head and point it out.* Like that would stop him from claiming the forfeit though.

In his thoughts, the tetchy one returned. She laughed and quietly advised him on what was allowed and what was not for such a boon. No death to another, no attack on the one charged with the forfeit, no stealing or other immoral requests, no stupid and frivolous wishes for wealth or beauty. Mentally he gave her a little nudge letting her know enough was enough already. She chuckled and gave him a mental swat on his arm before she withdrew, amused and not at all offended. Lance thought he might have liked her under other circumstances. She reminded him of Tilly before the accident. He tilted his head and looked over at the ladies, but he couldn't tell which one she was by looking at them; other than the one that spoke, their features were shrouded as if behind a thin veil. Curious and unsettling. Still, he carefully considered what she'd told him and what to ask.

"Thank you, Lady Morrigan. My boon request is: return to us the ancient dagger that the *Dubh Fae* stole from me."

She gave an acknowledging smile but her eyes remained hard.

"Granted."

Even as she spoke, the dagger took form in the air before him, right past the shore of Avalon. Lance grabbed for the hilt and his hand passed right through as the illusion plummeted down. He glared at the Morrigan.

She sniffed back and turned away from him as if he were of little consequence. "Your business here is done, follow the guide and you will claim your boon," she cast over her shoulder. Her hand traced a complicated pattern through the air.

Lance marveled that he could see it. As the world suddenly went odd, his tetchy lady spoke again in his head: *Hold fast to your friends, my prionsa. So much power among the elementals; and you, in part of mortal flesh, so seemingly frail in comparison, you encompass them all. Do not forget.* This time a phantom kiss brushed his cheek, leaving Lance very confused.

To a rolling peal of thunderclaps and the raucous cry of a thousand crows, Lance and his companions swirled away like mist on the wind.

Five lightning bolts struck the ground in front of *Delilah's* amid the echo of crows cawing. As the electric glow, Lance and the Four Winds appeared at the points of impact. A faint scorched odor hung in the air and every nerve ending tingled as Lance forced hyper-tense muscles to ease. He glanced over at the others, taking stock. For the most part, they appeared okay. Enlil seemed a little overcharged, while Anatu looked drained and Enki a bit fried, but they already shook it off. A glance at Nur and Lance had to laugh; the bastard grinned as if it tickled. All were relatively safe and accounted for.

Before they caught their breath, reality sundered. Just at the edge of the property, where the road met the gravel parking lot, a crude gate ripped open from the faerie realm. No finesse, no skill, just brutal power shredding its way through.

Nur whistled low and long. "Damn, that lady's got her timing down...look what's coming."

Lance readied for a fight, gathering in magic, unsheathing his knife, and making sure the thunderbolt was accessible. To either side of him he felt the Winds likewise prepare. Enki sheathed his fists in gauntlets carved from pure granite, yet somehow as supple as Lance's new leathers. Anatu wielded a bullwhip of harnessed riptide; Enlil a quarterstaff shaped of the hardest edge of the arctic wind, and Nur...Nur was on fire. It danced in his eyes, spouted from the rough patch on his forehead and trailed down both arms and beyond until there were flaming blades in place of his hands. He didn't need a weapon; he was a weapon. Lance quirked a brow.

"What? Too over the top?" Mischief danced among the flame in Nur's gaze as he spoke. The others laughed and the growing tension eased—as Lance suspected the South Wind had intended. As everyone loosened up, Nur toned it back until only his eyes and rough patch flickered, conserving his flame.

The *Dubh Fae* tumbled from the gate as graceless as ever. Blood ran down his face and his left wing fin appeared completely gone. He staggered across the gravel lot toward where they stood, only to collapse fifteen feet away.

"What the hell?" Lance murmured with a scowl on his face. Nur shrugged, but Lance already knew, though it took him a moment to recognize what he actually saw: The *Dubh Fae* fled before the faerie horde. At the fore, clad in his leather armor and swaggering like some thug out of a Quentin Tarantino movie, was the *Ard Ri*'s knight, Callan.

"Well, damn," Nur murmured. "Guess they found some rope." It didn't matter how the *Ard Ri*'s forces made it down off the clouds; they were here and clearly spoiling for a fight.

Lance and the Winds stepped forward, weapons at the ready, as the door to *Delilah's* smacked open and those left behind to guard the families poured out...including Suzanne. Lance cursed, but didn't order any of them back; this is what they'd been left here for, after all. It just meant one thing: he had to end this quickly.

Lance called out to Enlil, pointing to where the *Ard Ri*'s forces still marched through the gate: "Take that down!" With a violent, pinpoint whirlwind the East Wind disrupted the fabric of the portal, trapping those still in faerie on the other side. But even at half-strength, the fae forces outnumbered the bikers.

The lot looked like a scene out of Sons of Anarchy meets Lord of the Rings. Bikers in leather, armed with knives, chains, pipes, or whatever else came to hand, faced off against nearly every creature from myth and legend, imagined and unimagined, armed with swords and blades and any number of weapons Lance couldn't identify.

He hauled in mage energy and palmed his bowie knife.

Both forces stood there unmoving for a long moment as the *Dubh Fae* sprawled across the gravel like a bone between two packs of dogs, each side trying to get a read on the other.

Delilah's didn't have any close neighbors. Good thing.

The moment passed.

A free-for-all ensued as each side flung itself at the other, unleashed at some unspoken signal. Screams and curses sent the birds scattering from the nearby trees. They added their cries to the ruckus. Steel rang against fae metal and fist slapped flesh. The crunch of gravel ran like a pulse beneath it all.

To Lance's left, Mongo and Garm tore into a fae with dripping green hair and what looked like a massive claymore. The dog darted in to nip as his owner whipped out the anchor chain that usually kept the hound secure. Spinning it like a bolo Mongo wrapped it around his opponent's wrist, the one holding the sword, and yanked, disarming him.

Off to the right Suzanne put the Bride from *Kill Bill 2* to shame, whupping ass and not bothering with names. Just past her, though, Davey took a beating from something that looked like a bear with a bull's head, until Irish and a couple of others drove the creature back.

Lance didn't leap in right away, other than to smack down those brave enough to come at him. Magic or blade or fist, he wielded all three with a single-minded focus intended only to clear his way. He kept his eye on the Dubh Fae, or more accurately the dagger sheathed at the faerie's side. Reaching out with his magic, Lance made a grab for the blade, only to have the effort shoved aside. He looked up and came eye to eye with Callan, likewise converging on the prize.

Snarling, Lance lashed out again, this time at the *Ard Rí's* flunky. Callan reeled from the impact but kept on coming, pretty much ignoring the mage attack. As he advanced, the blade slid from the *Dubh Fae's* sheath. There was no way Lance would let him have that dagger. Callan expected a magical attack, so Lance got creative. Drawing back his right foot, he kicked forward with the side of it like he was kicking a soccer ball, digging into the gravel, sending it flying into the dark elf's face. An annoyance more than anything, but enough of a distraction that the dagger fell back to the ground.

"That is *mine*, Abomination," the warrior growled.

"Interesting choice of words," Lance called back, sensing the insurrection in the fae ranks. "What does your *king* think about that?"

Callan didn't answer. Verbally.

Lance braced for the coming smack-down. He greedily drew in energy until his wings snapped out behind him with the speed of a fire hose filling with water. He raised his shields and found his balance, then ran forward to take the offensive before Callan could strike. He barely noticed as the Winds bracketed him like an honor guard, taking out anyone coming at him from the sides. Lance remained focused on the mage bolt forming in his thoughts, watching as it slammed down on the fae.

Callan's expression turning to granite, he lashed out with a blast of his own, simultaneously reinforcing his shields. Back and forth they went, trading blasts until Lance burnt off enough steam to see they weren't getting anywhere but exhausted. He stopped and switched to thinking with his forebrain. With a wisp of energy, he visualized a shield unlike any other, inverted and slick on the inside. He held it cupped outward until Callan sent through another blast, then slipped it around his adversary.

And for a blessed moment, peace.

The shield reflected Callan's efforts inward, cutting him off from any additional source of magic and for at least the moment holding him physically in place. Lance stalked forward, and scooped up the faerie dagger that had started this all. Callan went wild. He rammed the shield until it shifted, not letting him loose, but no longer anchoring him. The fae then tensed and strained. His eyes narrowed and his head tilted. An unholy expression transformed his face as a glimmer of satisfaction creeping in gaze. His eyes closed and he went inexplicably still. Lance fell back, guardedly watching for the attack so he could counter.

Lance lost sight of one thing...pissing off warriors, they didn't just glare or toss a punch. They rained down retribution.

Another mage bolt hammered down, followed by a shitstorm of similar blows. As Lance dodged and scrambled to evade the attack, he saw his mistake. The shield spell cut the fae off from mundane magic, but gave him a protected space to tap the land of faerie.

Crap! Only...Lance suddenly remembered a certain tetchy voice and her parting advice, triggered by the fae's innovation. The Four Winds were elementals, not fae. His faceless friend made a point of the fact that Lance, being part mortal, was comprised of all the elements. The possibilities were...damn... they were beyond brutal, in a good way. If this worked. If Lance didn't fry himself in the attempt. Dodging more blows, he sent up the hand signal specific to the Winds, calling them together. They scrambled and reached his side even as Callan unleashed a blast that rattled Lance's brains. He shook it off and reached for Nur's hand.

"Quick, link up."

He'd seen the Winds do this before, but he'd never been in the mix. Grasping each other forearm to forearm, they formed a bond like nothing he'd ever felt in his life. Lance took it in his mental grip and bent his will on deepening it, drawing energy from the whole as if from himself. Another blow came and Lance nearly lost the meld until Anatu brought her focus to the fore, and then likewise did the others, forming a shield. Lance's body arched with the magic he tried to harness and he began to wonder how stupid this really was as the flood of energy very nearly shattered his brain.

He sent rapid-fire strikes toward the stunned Callan, their intensity leaving Lance himself scorched. Determined, he kept it up, though, until the fae and his forces fell back and the invading fae fled Underhill.

Quickly, before the remaining energy incinerated them, Lance dumped it, forcing it out through the nearest channel that did not lead to one of the Winds.

And discovered something else....

They had pulled the *Dubh Fae* into the meld. Just a loose link, likely engaged out of proximity, triggered by Lance's earlier focus forming an unintentional bond. By the time he realized where the channel led, Lance had poured the energy that threatened to consume him and the Winds through that bond.

Kerwin's death-cry screamed through them, echoing off the souls of fae and mortal alike. Though only loosely bonded to them, Kerwin's passing shot deep down in the foundation of the melding until Lance and the Winds collapsed to the gravel, their own systems carrying a piece of the death.

Lance would never forget that scream.

Long moments passed before they came back to themselves. When they did, they all spoke at once. "Fuck. Oh shit." With difficulty, they hauled themselves off the ground and helped as the Wild Hunt started to clean up. Lance's thoughts remained elsewhere, though.

The *Dubh Fae*'s death didn't particularly upset him in itself, not after all the attacks and everything else that had happened. Not after what the fae had done to Suzanne...But the way it went down, that ate at him like battery acid. There was nothing righteous in taking out someone beaten and down, no matter that it was unintentional. If anything, that made it worse. What if the one to die had been someone he actually gave a damn about? Someone who meant something, like Tilly, or Suzanne? Lance needed to learn how to handle this magic before he did more damage. But there wasn't time for that, not until this was done.

This wasn't done until they had Tilly back.

"Fuck," Lance swore more softly as he entered *Delilah's*. Everyone sat in stunned silence. Bad enough he saw wounded everywhere, worse to see the shrouded mounds stretched out on the bar. They'd lost at least two of their own. Fuck. *Fuck.* His control slipped just a little. Suzanne came over but he couldn't let her touch him, not without losing it, not with the *Dubh Fae* still screaming deep inside him and the realization fresh in his mind that it could have been her.

As he stepped out of reach and addressed the room Lance felt something hard take hold of him inside. He let it.

"I'm going to get Tilly."

"You will *all* stay here." Residual magic buzzed around him as he stared down the stunned looks from those around him. No one argued.

Lance handed the dagger they'd fought for to Nur for safe keeping and slid his uncle's dagger through his belt. He wasn't stupid enough to return the real thing. The blades were near enough in feel and appearance that he hoped Dair wouldn't have time to realize the deception.

He gave his uncle a hard stare over his shoulder on his way out.

"I have one question for you, *Jonraphal*—what are you hiding from me?"

Jon's expression flashed with pain, which he quickly buried. Lance nodded slowly. He hadn't expected anything different but he was more than a little fed up with such secrecy from family.

"Until you're ready to answer that question you need to steer clear of me."

Without another word Lance pulled a mage veil over himself and vanished from sight and sound.

Alone, armed with the decoy dagger and nothing more, Lance stalked out to the wold behind *Delilah's* and walked until he encountered a faerie ring, not too far in . Stepping to the center of the mushroom circle Lance unleashed a tendril of magic and opened up a pinhole in the ether. Through the hole he extended his senses into the fae realm and searched for the tell-tale tugging so new to him. He focused on the link that spoke of family bonds and reached.

After all, blood called to blood.

The magic connected and Lance opened the portal further. Stepping through, he followed the tug of kinship right into the ravaged Hall of the *Ard Ri.* If not for the magnificent living throne Gavin had described, Lance would never have recognized where he was. The trees were tattered and the place desolate. It felt more like a derelict than a thriving seat of power. The faint smell of leaf mold hung in the air, lurking among motes of dust, and there were signs of neglect everywhere. The absence of any courtiers spoke more loudly than anything of Dair na Scath's decline. The Hall seemed deserted save for a single, brooding figure hunched on the throne, oblivious to Lance's presence.

No one else was in the room. *No one.*

Still enshrouded by magic, Lance covered every inch of the Hall looking for a hidden chamber, or magical pocket, somewhere—anywhere—Tilly might be stashed. The entire time he searched, Lance felt tethered, the blood link tugging and tugging and tugging, from a steady point at his back.

He turned and stalked to the dais until he stood five feet from the throne.

And the truth could not be denied.

"They should have told me," he ground out past clenched teeth.

Lance had been too angry, too distracted to notice at their previous encounter: in the Ard Ri's face he saw faint traces of his own features, a fact that made him both sick and furious on so many levels. Grandfather? Uncle? Some other such relative twice removed? Like it mattered when the guy wanted Lance dead. What did matter is that Jon and Delilah should have told him instead of leaving him clueless! Logic told him they'd done it to protect him, but right now, logic wasn't worth shit. It was too much. Way too much on top of all that just happened.

He lost control of the scream clawing at his gut.

Dair did not react at all.

Lance discovered something else: this king was broken, both his mind and his strength, completely unaware that someday soon Callan would likely tear away his throne. Lance couldn't care less. He was fed up with the Fae Court and Underhill, the *Ard Ri* and subterfuge.

This was not his world.

He reached up with his left hand and his will to grip the veil shielding him. Slowly he pulled it away and stood there bared to sight, both magical and otherwise. In his right hand rested Jon's ancient blade, masquerading as the one too many had died for. Lance raised it up high, making sure the Ard Ri couldn't get a really good look.

The fae's eyes flared bright, and then dimmed erratically. A muscle in his cheek spasmed as he came to his feet, fear and outrage and pure, black hatred coming off him in waves. The madness Gort had warned about overshadowed all else.

Lance wasn't in any mood for insane ranting. Envisioning his fist closing tight around the *Ard Ri*'s throat, enough to still his voice but not his breath—though that too was tempting—Lance released a bit of magic to make it so.

The king surged forward. Gesturing with his hand as his wings unfurled. With a sneer, Lance drew back with the dagger, ready to end it, blood kin or not. The *Ard Ri* halted, trembling where he stood, but not in fear. He acted like a barely controlled beast, every muscle straining with the need to leap forward. Lance knew how he felt.

"Do you know me, Dair na Scath?"

His face twisted and dark, the High King slowly nodded.

"Do you know this blade?"

Again he nodded.

"Good, then listen to me closely, *Grandfather*." That guess was as good as any. Lance's voice dipped low and deep and lethal as he mounted the steps of the dais, easy strides taking him right up into the *Ard Ri*'s face. "I wanted nothing of this land, of my birthright. I did not even know I had claim to your throne. You changed all that. *You.* So understand this, unless you give me my cousin, now, I will take this blade and prick my own hand. I will spill my blood onto your fucking throne and twice bind myself to it: by virtue of my blood and by the portion of my mother, *Anaiphal*, alive within me." There was a vicious grin on Lance's face. He could feel it. "Do you understand me, *A Shoilse*?" Lance demanded, sarcasm heavy in the address.

Dair na Scath screamed silently with rage and lunged for the dagger. In an instant Lance had flooded his wings with energy until the size of them well surpassed Dair's own. He used the barest bit of the magic to shove the fae right back on his ass into the throne.

"Let me make myself clear, I do not want your rule, but I damn well will take it. Unless. You. Give. Her. Back. NOW!"

A shudder. A flinch. And the old fae broke. Tilly appeared in a shower of glittering dust motes, spell-bound but conscious. Lance caught her with his free hand and drew her tight against him, beneath his crackling wings. She stirred and looked up at him, eyes wide and her mouth gaping, as if she wanted to speak but couldn't for the spell. Trembling took him, so faint that only she could tell. Carefully, gently he brushed her with a thought and Dair's binding spell faded.

"Lance," she murmured urgently, in a grown voice not heard for many years, "I want to go home. Take me home."

He went dead still as he searched her face, her eyes, and saw what he never expected to see again. Reason. Joy rocked him, but he could not express it. Not here. He clenched his jaw against the jubilation he felt, shoving it deep before Dair read it as a weakness. He could not explain it, but Tilly was herself, clear-eyed and coherent as if her skull had never cracked open. And then he thought back to the encounter in Avalon: he'd willed away the cloud holding her bound. He had thought to banish Dair's control over her, but it seemed Lance had done much more.

Brushing a kiss across her forehead, he cast the decoy dagger at Dair's feet and met the faerie's eye with a promise more fierce than ever. "If you are wise, you will nod your head and *mean* it when I say you will leave me and mine alone."

The shattered King did so, and then turned his head aside, but not before Lance spied the calculating loathing in his gaze. Someday Dair na Scath would forget the oath, if he survived Callan's play for power. But not today.

Lance turned his back on the throne and murmured softly to Tilly, "Come on, we're going home."

With a show of might and a snap of his wings, Lance opened a gate right there in the Hall of the Ard Ri. On the far side he saw Suzanne waiting, a frown puckering her brow. Lance could no longer resist. As he stepped through the gate he let loose a triumphant cry that echoed long through the hall of the Faerie King.

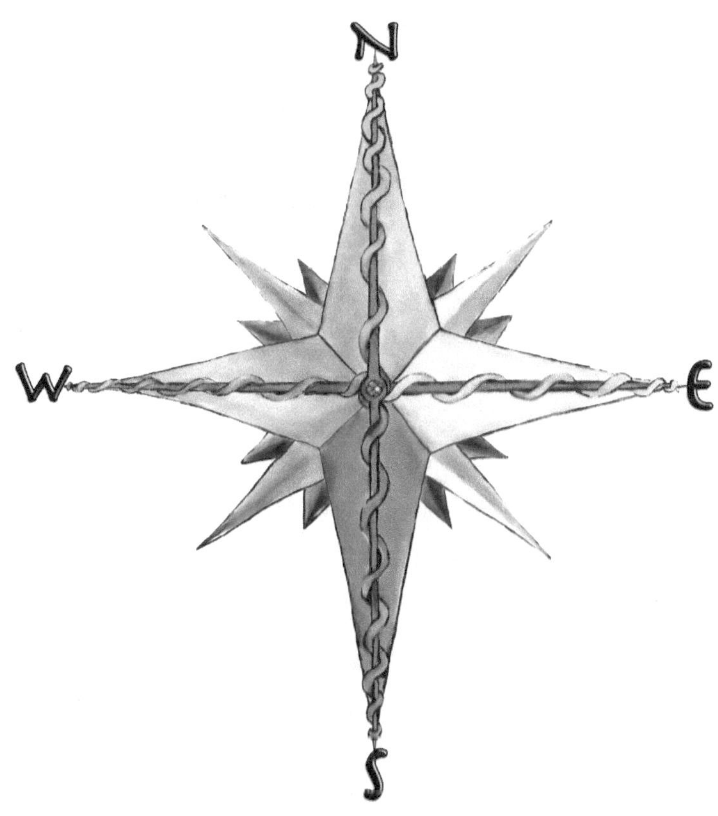

N
W
E
S

Dair na Scath

Glossary of Terms

A Shoilse – Irish Gaelic for "majesty."

Anatu – The name chose by the West Wind of the Wild Hunt; also called Ana. Variant spelling of Semitic (Ugaritic) Anat, meaning "water spring." In mythology, this is the name of a goddess of war, the sister and lover of the great storm god Ba'al. She is said to have been a consumer of blood and flesh.

Avalon – The legendary resting place of King Arthur where he went to heal after his battle with Mordred. Though tied to the British myth, Avalon is said to be in many places around the world and connected with several different myth cycles.

Bean Sidhe – Irish Gaelic for "woman of the hills," in Celtic tradition such women announced when someone was about to die. Sometimes only their wailing was heard, and other times they were seen washing bloody garments in the river. When the death was of a great leader, several bean sidhe would pronounce the death. The term has been Anglicized to banshee.

Bike Lane – The center line in the road, between lanes where there is enough room between the opposing traffic for a bike to zip through.

'Blood Band – A magical ring of the author's creation, worn by those of *Rudha-an* royal blood to protect them from magical attack. The ring bonds to the flesh and cannot be removed.

BUG – Big Ugly Guy, a big hostile person.

Cage – A car or other four-wheeled vehicle where the drivers and passengers are closed in.

Cager – Someone that drives a car.

Callan – The champion of the faerie court and aspirer to the throne.

Cherry-top – A police car.

Church – Club meetings.

Citizen – Anyone who is not a member of a Biker Organization.

Colors – The patch signifying the motor club or organization a biker is affiliated with.

Coupons – Speeding tickets.

Dair na Scath – Irish Gaelic for "Shadow Oak" or "Oak of Shadow" – The king of the High Court, Lance's grandfather.

Donor Card – Put someone into a state where their donor card can be collected.

Dragon's Tears – A fictional corrosive fluid devised by the author for the purpose of the story, it is unclear if it is or is not the actual tears of dragons, but undiluted it will eat through anything but diamond.

Dubh Fae (The) – See Kerwin.

Dušan – The name the Four Winds gave to Lance. Czech name derived from the Slavic element *dusha*, meaning "soul, spirit."

Enki – The name chosen by the North Wind of the Wild Hunt. Sumerian meaning either "lord of the earth" or "lord of the underworld." In Babylonian mythology, this is the name of a god of creation, wisdom, keeper of divine laws, and half-brother to Enlil.

Endo – Stopping a motorcycle and having the rear wheel lift off the ground, a reverse of the catwalk. 2. Going back over front. 3. Pitching the rear of the motorcycle over its front, end over end.

Enlil – The name chosen by the East Wind of the Wild Hunt; also called Blow. Sumerian name meaning "Lord Wind," or more literally "Lord of the Command." In Babylonian mythology, this is the name of the chief deity and half-brother to Enki.

Fat Boy – First introduced in 1990, this cycle instantly became one of Harley-Davidson's most popular models. Originally available in only grey, later models came in any color except grey, including two-tone. The most distinguishing feature of this bike is the 16-inch solid wheels used both front and rear; it remains the only model so equipped. They ride the Softail frame, which hides the shocks beneath the engine. Power by an 80-cubic-inch Evolution V-twin introduced six years earlier, the Fat Boy uses belt drive.

Fluid Exchange – Biker term for a pit stop where the gas tank is filled and the bladder drained.

Front Door – The lead position on a run.

Gavin – Full fae, brother to Suzanne, Lance's lieutenant and best friend, member the mother chapter of the Wild Hunt.

Gremlin – Mischievous, mechanical-oriented fae often associated with the air force and blamed for plane malfunctions (Also see Road Gremlin).

Guardian Bell/Ride Bell/Gremlin Bell – Stems from an actual biker legend, a pewter or brass bell hung from a bike as protection from road gremlins. If the gremlin is already on the bike, the ringing of the bell traps it within the bell until it becomes senseless and falls off. If the gremlin is trying to get on the bike, the ringing scares it away. The magic of the bell is said to double if it is presented as a gift by a loved one.

Hose Your Ride – To wear out or damage a bike.

Keep the dirty side down – drive safe and keep the bike in the proper, upright position. The rest of the phrase is "keep the shiny side up."

Kerwin – The Little Black One – Also known at the *Dubh Fae*, the Black Faerie, another halfling, only one whose fae nature was dominant over his mortal half.

Knucklehead – A type of Harley-Davidson engine munufactured prior to 1948, which was characterized by large nuts on the right side of engine above the cylinders. Appearance is somewhat similar to knuckles. 2. Slang of Harley-Davidson Knucklehead engine (V-Twin, produced from 1936 - 1947). Name comes from the valve covers that look like the knuckles of a clinched fist. 3. Harley-Davidson's first overhead valve Big Twin.

Lance – Leader of the Wild Hunt, Suzanne's mate, best friend to Gavin, founding member of the Wild Hunt, also called Dušan by the Four Winds.

Leathers – The protective gear worn by bikers, could mean jacket, vest, gauntlets, chaps.

Lone Wolf Biker – Someone who lives the Bike Lifestyle but chooses not to ride with a club.

Love Nudges – Also known as swapping paint. Two riders bump in to each other while racing.

Mama – A woman that is available to all members of the club for sexual favors.

Mamó – Irish Gaelic for grandmother.

Mattress Cover – A young, pretty woman.

MC – Motor Club, biker gang.

Megatron – Speeds in excess of 150mph.

Meth – Methamphetamine, often abused drug that rapidly releases dopamine in reward regions of the brain producing the intense euphoria, or "rush," that many users feel after snorting, smoking, or injecting the drug.

Nur – The name chosen by the South Wind of the Wild Hunt; also called Bubba. Aramaic name meaning "fire."

Old Lady – A biker's wife or steady girlfriend.

1%er – Outlaw bikers, those one percent of the biker population that give the rest a bad name.

Open the Throttle/Throttle Down – Control the intake of air and fuel entering the engine to go faster or slower.

Organ Donor – Reckless biker, likely to get themselves and/or others killed, bikers that ride without a helmet.

Originals – A member's first set of colors which are never to be cleaned.

Panhead – A Harley-Davidson motorcycle engine, so nicknamed because of the distinct shape of the valve-rocker covers. The engine is a two-cylinder, two-valve-per-cylinder, pushrod V-twin. The engine replaced the Knucklehead engine in 1948 and was manufactured until 1965 when it was replaced by the shovelhead.

Patch Holder – Member of a motorcycle club.

Pillion pad – The passenger seat.

Pooka – A shape-shifting fae that can take many forms but is most well-known for appearing as a horse. If a human should mount one, it has been known to give them a wild ride, but do no real harm.

Q-tip – An old, white or blue-haired driver, considered unpredictable and dangerous to others on the road.

Rat Bike – An older bike that hasn't been taken care of.

Redcap – Malevolent, murderous fae that dye their signature red caps in the blood of their victims.

Ride – Slang term for a motorcycle.

Ride Captain – The person in charge of a ride or road trip.

Road Agent – Another term for Highway Patrol Officer or State Trooper.

Road Gremlin/Gremlin – The evil spirits of the road that cause accidents and mechanical problems. Akin to the gremlins said to plague the air force pilots, who formed the first motor clubs. Gremlins like to ride. By hanging a bell on the bike a rider can either keep the gremlins from getting on, or trap them if they are already there, preventing them from causing mischief and damage to the bike or rider.

Rudha-an Tree – Gaelic for rowan tree, also called mountain ash, Whispering tree, or Witch wood tree, among many other things. Many of these can be easily linked to the mythology and folklore surrounding the tree. The small, creamy white flowers are borne in dense corymbs. The fruit is a small pome, usually bright orange or red, but occasionally pink, yellow or white in some Asian species. It was thought to be a magical tree and protection against malevolent beings.

Scoot – Slang term for a motorcycle.

Shoulder Fin – Author's creation for the purpose of the story. The anatomical feature that expands as the fae draw on magic. Something like a heat sink, it channels the magical energy into harmless tendrils that expand and resemble wings. This protects the fae from magical overload or burnout until the energy is used.

Shovelhead – Slang for Harley-Davidson engines produced between 1966 and 1984, so named because of the shape of the head resembles a coal shovel. The Shovelhead engine (V-Twin, produced from 1966- 1984). Harley-Davidson's third generation overhead valve Big Twin engine.

Sidhe na Daire – Irish Gaelic for Elf or hill of the oak. For the purpose of the story, Dair na Scath's fortress Underhill.

Softtail – Harley frame with hidden suspension; resembles a hard tail.

SQUID – SQuirrely kID – An inexperienced young biker trying to ride beyond their skill level, often with no respect for the posted speed limit or safety, their own or others. Possibly a Southern term.

Statey – State troopers or police.

Static – A run in with the police.

Stay Vertical – Stay upright, don't crash.

Steel Horse Stampede – Where hundreds of bikers ride *en masse* down to Lynchburg, TN for a biker rally.

Surf the Asphalt – laying the bike down in a skid.

Suzanne – Lance's woman, full fae, sister to Gavin, member of mother chapter of the Wild Hunt.

Sweep – The last position in a ride formation, generally assigned to the best and most trusted rider.

Tar Snake – Thick lines of uneven tar used to repair cracks in the road, a hazard to bikers.

Tat/Skin Art/Ink – Tattoo.

Team - A subgroup of four motorcycles within a larger group ride.

Thunderbolt – An expanding metal baton.

Tri-Armor – A brand of extremely strong protective biker gear.

Two Up – A term for carrying a passenger on the back of the bike.

Underhill – The land of the Faeries. Not always literally under a hill, but called so because of the time long ago when the Fae were force to live underground, away from mortals.

War Wagon – A vehicle use to haul a biker club's arsenal when trouble is expected from another club.

Wind Walker – A respected biker that looks out for others on the road.

Wrench – A bike mechanic.

References

http://www.custom-choppers-guide.com/biker-gangs.html
http://www.totalmotorcycle.com/dictionary/motorcycle-dictionary-index.htm
http://en.wikipedia.org/wiki/Motorcycle_club
http://www.nida.nih.gov/InfoFacts/methamphetamine.html
http://www.20000-names.com/element_names.htm
http://invisibledoor.com/paganman/elements/elements.html elements
http://en.wikipedia.org/wiki/Panhead
http://en.wikipedia.org/wiki/Rowan

Danielle Ackley-McPhail

An award-winning author and editor, Danielle has worked both sides of the publishing industry for longer than she cares to admit. In 2014 she joined forces with husband Mike McPhail and friend Greg Schauer to form her own publishing house, eSpec Books.

Her published works include six novels, *Yesterday's Dreams, Tomorrow's Memories, Today's Promise, The Halfling's Court, The Redcaps' Queen,* and *Baba Ali and the Clockwork Djinn,* written with Day Al-Mohamed. She is also the author of the solo collections *A Legacy of Stars, Consigned to the Sea, Flash in the Can,* and *Transcendence,* the non-fiction writers' guide, *The Literary Handyman,* and is the senior editor of the *Bad-Ass Faeries* anthology series, *Gaslight & Grimm, Dragon's Lure,* and *In an Iron Cage.* Her short stories are included in numerous other anthologies and collections.

Danielle lives in New Jersey with husband and fellow writer, Mike McPhail and three extremely spoiled cats. She can be found on Facebook (Danielle Ackley-McPhail) and Twitter (DMcPhail, BadAssFaeries, eSpecBooks, and TheHornieLady).

To learn more about her work, visit:

www.sidhenadaire.com
www.especbooks.com
www.badassfaeries.com.

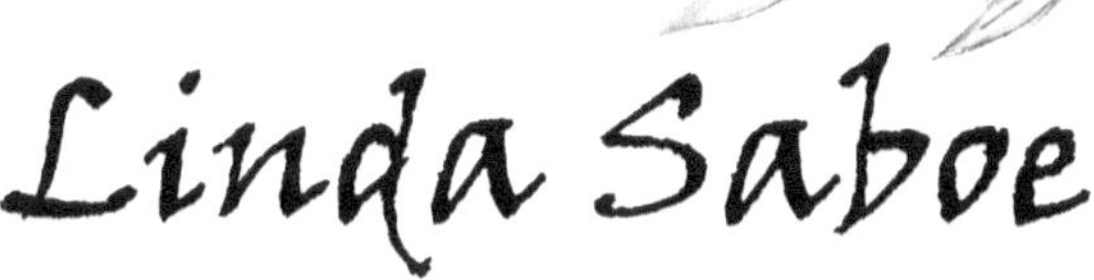

Linda Saboe

LINDA STARTED TO DRAW SERIOUSLY AT AGE TWO, CONTINU-
ing on until it became apparent that her children en-
joyed eating on a regular basis. So she got a job. Now
that her children can feed themselves, she quit the job
and started drawing again.

Linda works in oil paints, paper and digital drawing,
polymer clay and, most recently, rabbits. She is the il-
lustrator of *The Evil Gazebo* and *The Halfling's Court*.

She does not enjoy writing bios.

To see more of her work, visit www.croneswood.com.

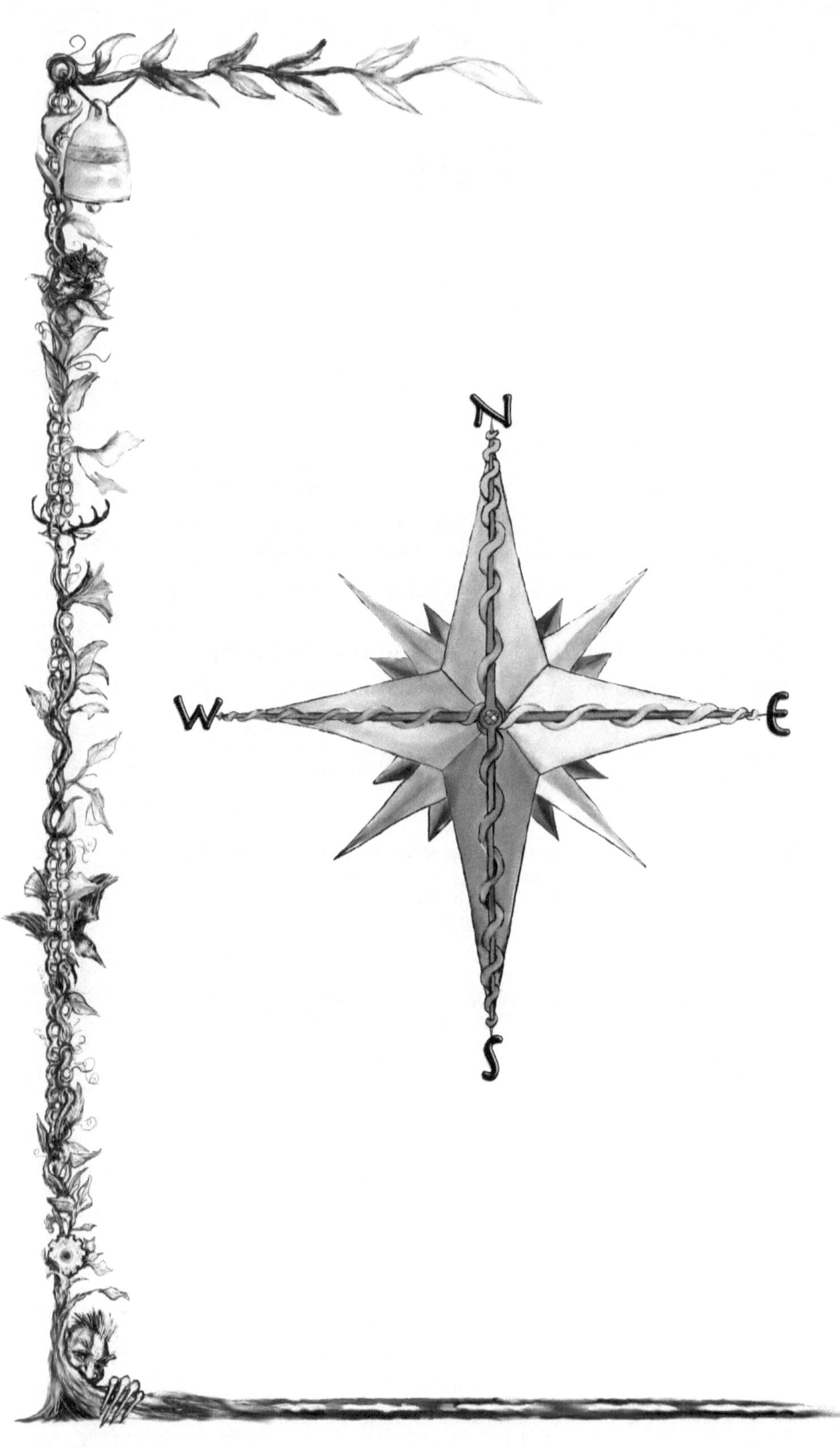

N
W
E
S

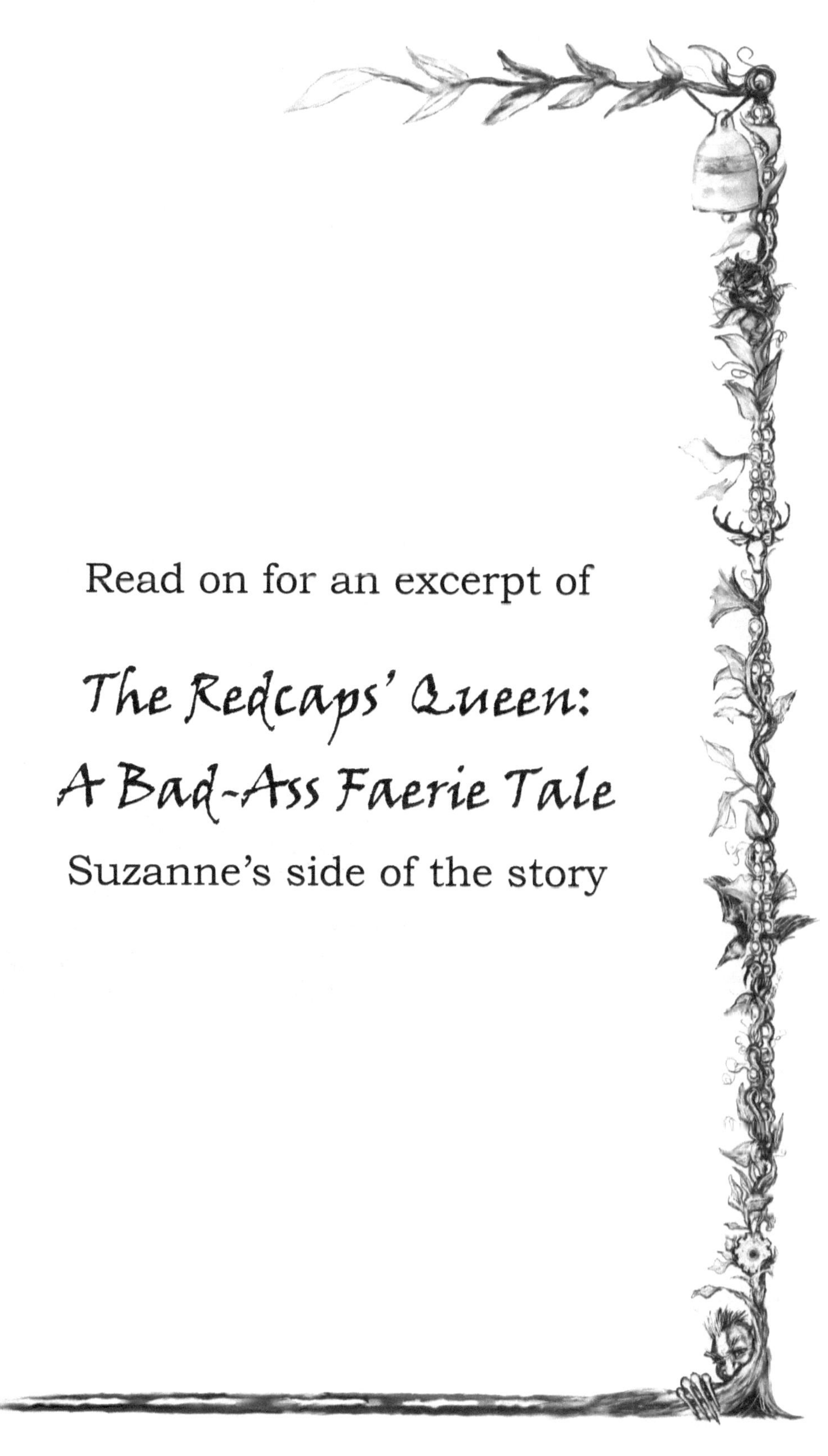

Read on for an excerpt of

The Redcaps' Queen:
A Bad-Ass Faerie Tale
Suzanne's side of the story

Chapter One

Suzanne surfaced to the sounds of softly rustling *leaves. The raucous cawing of crows. And sinister murmurs close by her ear. The chill of a breeze tickled her bare back as the sharp pain of bindings on her wrists and legs kindled anger in her breast.*

The impulse to fight surged strongly within her, yet something more than physical bonds held her immobile. Her effort to open her eyes triggered no more than a weak flutter. The blackness briefly lightened to grey before darkening once more. Inwardly, Suzanne growled, drew several deep, centering breaths, and once more bent her will toward moving.

Nothing.

The murmurs increased. She couldn't distinguish what they said, but their growing excitement needed no words. Many hands grasped her. Lifted her up. Bore her away. Suzanne threw her effort into resisting as what felt like sharp-pointed claws pierced her flesh. Her mind fought, but her body remained lax. Her breathing labored the more she strained internally against the force that bound her. The rasp of something like barbed sandpaper swiped across her bare shoulder. Her stomach twitched at the sensation and her muscles screamed to break free of her bonds. Suzanne's pulse picked up and her frustration grew. The more anxious she became the more the fog cleared from her mind.

And then she felt him.

Lance, her lover, was somewhere nearby. The spell she had forged to link them trickled his emotions into her thoughts. Love. Concern. Anger. The last most of all; his temper boiled fierce and hot beneath his skin, even in the bare echo that she felt through their magical bond. Suzanne's soul reached for him but found itself likewise bound. Panic flooded her veins, born of memories long past of childhood beneath her father's control. Kept weak and powerless, her every act dictated. In the here-and-now, Suzanne's breath came in sharp gasps. The darkness deepened until she grew frantic, casting her inner self once more against restraints she could not shake free.

Someone spoke. Distant, yet all too clear. A flat, harsh voice, reminiscent of the crows' caws.

"Service rendered calls for payment due."

Her bearers lowered her to the ground and backed away. Like a rabbit sensing the hawk that circled overhead, her inner self stilled, unsure of how to evade.

"No!" Lance roared.

The world came clear as the esoteric restraints lifted. In the next instant, bitter-cold droplets struck Suzanne's skin. Acid burrowed deep and fast to devour her flesh. No longer weighed down, she bucked and thrashed. Her eyes snapped open. The clawed hands returned, pinning her down, and her vision filled with wizened faces beneath brown caps that deepened to crimson as her blood flowed and the redcaps feasted.

Suzanne screamed a piercing, earth-ending scream.

She jerked awake, sweat-soaked, her body trembling and her breath fast and shallow in reaction to the raw, brutal memory haunting her dreams. Screams still echoed in her mind. Torturous, agonized, piercing. Lance lay undisturbed beside her, arm draped over her waist, breathing in a slow, relaxed rhythm against the back of her neck. His presence calmed her, again a reminder she'd survived. Most mornings were the same lately. Ever since she had been captured by the *Dubh Fae* and his redcap minions—coming within seconds of death—her sleep had been a stalking ground.

She growled in frustration as she edged away from Lance's loose grip. A grey hint of light placed the time somewhere just before dawn. Way too early to be up. She ignored the phantom, jabbing pains as she slipped from the bed. The chill of the morning air made her shiver as she ran her fingers over naked skin that should have borne scars. She caught her unblemished reflection in the bureau mirror across the room and shivered again. Damp tendrils of platinum-blonde hair clung to her face, neck, and breasts. In the low light, her blue eyes shone dark and startling against her ashen skin. She scowled at her reflection and quickly shimmied into her clothes, reflexively sliding a well-worn bandana in the front pocket of her jeans, an old habit from her childhood.

Behind her, Lance stirred. His arm reached for her in his sleep. The hint of a frown furrowed his brow. Awake or not, his protective nature seeped through. As the leader of the Wild Hunt M.C. he considered himself responsible for every member, but most particularly for her.

Again, frustration burned along her nerves, causing her to tense as she willed him to remain asleep. She loved Lance, had for over twenty years...even before he turned thirteen and discovered the joy of girls, but he never seemed to get the fact that she needed to stand on her own, not because she *had* to, but because it was important to her to be *able* to. She'd even held a job once. For nearly a year she'd manned the drying furnace at the local auto plant, where intense heat baked the fresh paint into a protective shell. A very unfae occupation; that had been part of its charm. With a whole other world of resources to draw on she hadn't needed to work. What she had needed was to prove she could. That she was strong and capable in all things. Not until she proved that to herself and everyone else, could she and Lance move forward and build the kind of life she had always longed for. The life where they were never separate, where family meant love...and children.

That dream seemed even further out of reach now. If only she could conquer this crippling fear. In the military they called it PTSD—post-traumatic stress disorder. Suzanne...she called it fucked up. Just seeing the color red froze her up worse than a seized engine. If she did not overcome that fear on her own, she expected she never would. But Lance kept interfering. He just never seemed to know when to stand down and when it was okay to step in. When he'd learned about her recent issues, he'd actually gone so far as to try and ban anything red from *Delilah's*, the bar that served as club house for the Wild Hunt. Well-intentioned as she recognized the effort to be, she stopped him straight away. Besides being impractical, a solution like that threatened to cripple her for good. Remnants of an older fear rose up at that thought. She would let no one make her weak again. *No one.*

As she stood there trying to rally for the day, the room around her took on a steadily growing red tinge reflected from the rising sun. Suzanne tensed and refused to close her eyes against the sight. She fought to get control of the panic, resisting the urge to crawl back into Lance's arms and pretend herself safe. She wouldn't do it, though; she made a point of never lying, as her father did, even to herself. The faster her heart beat, the more her skin crawled, as if distant eyes watched her, waiting eagerly for the chance to bleed her. Surrounded by the dawn's haze she relived the attack; the flood of red light swept her back to the blasted crossroads, bound and helpless as the *Dubh Fae's* Dragon Tears ate through her skin and flesh, and the redcaps feasted on her free-flowing blood. Suzanne shuddered. The panic gained ground until she nearly crumpled to the floor. Sheer will alone kept her standing tall, her slender frame too rigid now to tremble. An improvement after last night, where she'd been curled nearly fetal in Lance's arms, but still unacceptable. She reminded herself that those who had harmed her couldn't get past the shields safeguarding the property, including *Delilah's* and the living space above the bar.

It didn't help. The true demons lived in her head.

Deep beneath the trauma from the attack lurked her true fear: that her father was right. That she was weak and could not defend herself. She'd fought against those beliefs her whole life. That was likely the reason so many of her gifts to Lance— and anyone else she cared for—provided protection, right down to the magic tattoo of her likeness that linked their awareness. As if proving that she could take care of others meant she could look out for herself, too. Only...look how well she'd botched that.

Again Lance stirred in the bed behind her; he grumbled and came a little more awake. The flashback lost part of its grip on her as her thoughts latched on to him. His strength and presence tempted her to depend on him, to let him protect her. Furious with herself, she scrubbed her hand hard across tear-dampened cheeks.

Before he roused fully, Suzanne leaned over and tucked the warm blanket back around him, ran her hand gently over the soft waves of his light brown hair, lying long and loose over the pillow. "It's okay, babe," she murmured by his ear, a bit of magic giving weight to her words. Her heart surged and a smile crept across her lips. Impulse took her and she brushed a tender kiss across his brow. "Go back to sleep. I'm going downstairs."

She watched to make sure Lance drifted to sleep again before leaving the room. Grabbing her leather jacket from the closet by the apartment door, she carefully kept her eyes averted from the pile of winter gear on the shelf above it. The knit hats were a mix of all colors, but Lance's favorite—red— dominated. Suzanne shuddered as another flash of memory superimposed the leering, bloody face of a redcap over the pile of hats. Squeezing her eyes closed tight she yet again fought the anxiety the flashback caused. She stumbled back and the sleeve of her jacket caught on something. Opening her eyes, she saw an old air rifle with a blown gasket that Lance hadn't had the time to fix yet. Suzanne reached out, her hand lingering on the stock of the gun. An idea took root as she forced her gaze back to the pile of knit caps. Last night she'd told Lance she would handle this problem of hers...

Now seemed like a good time.

It took a massive effort to fight past her aversion, but she reached up and managed to pick through the jumble of winter hats. Her hand shook violently as she plucked out every red one she could find, shoving them into the sleeve of her jacket where she wouldn't see them until she had to.

Downstairs, in the back room of the bar, Delilah—Lance's aunt—kept an entire closet full of well-maintained paintball gear: from weapons and protection, to marker flags and CO_2 cartridges, not to mention a whole case of paintballs in ridiculous neon colors. That stockpile was the key to Suzanne's plan. Well, that, and the fact the Wild Hunt owned all the acreage within a two-mile radius of the bar.

She headed for Delilah's office to retrieve the ring of supply closet keys hanging just inside the door. She then returned to the back room and pulled all of the gear she wanted from the closet. Everything lay ready and waiting by the time the first footsteps sounded on the stairs. Jon, Lance's uncle and fellow exiled Fae, didn't appear surprised—by her or the pile of gear on the table—though the stack of stocking caps did seem to puzzle him a moment until he clued to the fact they were all red.

"Dušan doesn't have any idea what you're up to, does he?"

Her eyes narrowed. Jon rarely used the name the Four Winds had given Lance when the Hunt was formed; the subtle reminder that anyone wearing colors answered to him brought out her sense of rebellion. "You going to help, or get in the way?"

Jon's hands went up along with one corner of his mouth. "Me? I know better than that. S'long as you don't plan anything stupid, I got your back." He joined her at the table, picked up a Tippman pneumatic pistol, and made a show of inspecting it, then preparing it for use.

"You know, wanting to protect you isn't the same thing as thinking you aren't capable of protecting yourself," he finally said, without looking up from the airgun he loaded.

Suzanne ground her teeth as she glared at her hands. Her knuckles had gone white. She glanced back at Jon. "It's not what Lance thinks that I'm concerned about."

Across the table, Jon's head snapped up, a protest on his lips as he stared at her intently from beneath a shag of dark brown hair. His natural, deep purple highlights glimmered under the glamour that hid his magical state.

Before he could speak, Suzanne went on, her words hurried. "Or the Club...I'm the one that has to get my head on straight, before *I* start thinking I can't hack it."

Jon nodded slowly, his rich bronze-brown eyes fairly swirling in sympathetic memory. For a moment both of them remained silent as he held her gaze. Then Jon laid the readied pistol down and settled back in his chair.

"I understand," he said, and she could see he really did—both what she'd said, and what she hadn't—as plain as the haunted look in his eyes. They sat in taut silence as they waited for more bodies to arrive.

An odd group marched into the woods, decked out in assorted armor, with a hodge-podge of air weapons shoved into pockets or slung over shoulders. Suzanne had a handful of red canvas flags shoved in the right pocket of her leather jacket and a butterfly knife in the left...just in case. She cradled her airgun in her arms.

Behind and to her left followed Rock, Blow, Bubba, and Dream. They were known collectively as the Four Winds—she couldn't fathom why, for three were not of that aspect. Each was a powerful Elemental, respectively: Earth, Air, Fire, and Water. Along with Lance, they had founded the Wild Hunt M.C. They were kin to the Fae, but not of a kind. Most of her race had an affinity for one of the aspects, which drew them to the Elementals. But not Suzanne. If not for Lance, she would have had nothing to do with the four of them. She had something of an aversion. It wasn't personal; she was one of the rare faerie born of all four aspects—generally a mortal trait—a fact she'd grown up both hiding and hating. It had made growing up...difficult. She still hadn't gotten over that. Sometimes it proved an issue, but not today. Today their ambient strength grounded her.

On her right walked Jon and Delilah...her not quite technically in-laws, of a sort. She held them closer than family. She gained from them strength of a different variety, as one whose blood relatives—with the exception of her brother, Gavin—had only sought to undercut her confidence. Even after all her years in the Wild Hunt, Suzanne wasn't used to the support. She breathed deep into her belly and willed the tension out of her body on the exhale. Lance's aunt and uncle were nothing like her kin. She needed to remember that, instead of waiting for the proverbial knife in the back. Trying to shake off her nerves, she turned to Delilah. "Who's watching over Tilly?"

Tilly was Jon and Delilah's daughter and Lance's cousin. She was thirty-four—less than a year younger than Lance—but thanks to an Organ Donor who never should have been allowed on a bike, she wasn't quite right in the head anymore. She could function, but on the level of a four-year-old in a full-grown woman's body. After the accident Suzanne had given Tilly a crystal pendant to protect her from further harm, but the woman still needed someone to keep her out of mischief.

"Gort's keeping her company," Delilah answered, a slight frown on her face, as if she wasn't sure that was the best idea. "She's taken to him. Wouldn't settle in to her cartoons until we said her new friend could watch with her."

Now if that isn't interesting, Suzanne thought. *Imagine... the former advisor to the elven High King babysitting.* She had to chuckle as she pictured him parked on Delilah's couch with his brain leaking out his ear as Tilly ran through the worst that Disney XD had to offer. *Poor guy.*

Suzanne hadn't decided if she trusted the newest defector from the Fae Court, but Tilly's endorsement, believe it or not, counted as a mark in his favor. She didn't usually take to people she didn't know that quickly—even before the accident. And, if nothing else, Suzanne owed him for keeping the woman-child occupied and out of the way a while. Today would be much harder to pull off with Tilly underfoot. Bad enough Suzanne had already acquired an audience.

Bubba's wife, Samandrea, and their boys, Zack and Shawn, brought up the rear of their impromptu group. Suzanne could have done without them tagging along, but at least they were proving useful. Between them they hauled the extra gear. The boys came along strictly as spectators. Not only did Suzanne not want to have to pull her shots, but frankly, she couldn't take more of a blow to her confidence—the boys were too good at this. Sammy chose to sit it out to keep them in line, lest they forget they weren't participating.

Right now their number was uneven, but Suzanne had also texted Gavin. She found herself too edgy to wait for him to show, certain that Lance would come down any moment and either try to "help" or convince her that this wasn't necessary. Gavin knew where to go; he could catch up.

The deeper they went into the forest, the more Suzanne relaxed as dew-spangled grass slapped her ankles and the distant twittering of the morning birds welcomed her among the trees. She found more comfort here than anywhere else. A different kind of anticipation seeped into her gut; she could beat this...she *would* beat this psychological paralysis brought on by the color red, right here on her own turf.

"Hey! Hold up," a voice called across the back lot, from the direction of *Delilah's.* Suzanne turned around to look, walking backward, while the others glanced over their shoulders. Her brother's form appeared past the edge of the trees.

Gavin loped across the back field toward them, his dark blond hair hanging damp around his shoulders. Suzanne experienced a light jolt as he passed through the protections surrounding the land behind *Delilah's.* Only Club members and their families could cross the shield unaided. Gavin grinned at her as he went through, no doubt feeling the tingle of the magic on his skin. Suzanne laughed back, remembering when puberty had hit and they'd gotten giddy on running back and forth through the invisible curtain.

When her brother came close enough, Blow tossed a small ribbed cap at him, which he reflexively caught. The Wind Elemental wore a vicious grin on his narrow face as he quipped: "Last one here gets to play target!"

Gavin just shrugged and pulled the knit hat down over his ears as he turned to Suzanne, his green eyes still a little sleepy. "What's going on, *deifiúr?*"

She tensed again at his use of the Gaelic for sister, something he only did when he felt protective. Usually she hit him for it, but today she let it pass; not like she wouldn't be getting even. "Time for a little therapy," she answered.

His brows drew down in confusion, and his head gave a little tilt to the side. She hefted the airgun she'd armed herself with and pointed at the hat on his head. Understanding finally dawned. Gavin cursed half-heartedly but the love in his gaze made it clear he'd do anything for her, even play target. Long strides brought him to her side where he looked deep in her eyes, deep enough to make her shift her stance. In that instant, but for his coloring, he looked enough like their father that she unconsciously prepared to fight.

"Are you up for this?" he asked, his voice only loud enough for her. He did not mean it unkindly, but the question still battered her resolve. She wanted to say yes, but the word would not come.

As if mocking her, a crow cawed from nearby. Others answered all around, staccato, like a laugh ricocheting from tree to tree. The *Dubh Fae* had had a murder of crows with him the day Suzanne nearly died. The sound, combined with her brother's uncertainty, almost undid her.

It took an effort to keep her breath even, to not lose herself again in the memory. Her skin twitched as if beneath the weight of an unseen gaze. Gavin reached out and grasped her shoulder, steadying her. The faint doubt she had seen in his expression blossomed into full-blown concern. He knew what that day had done to her as no one other than Lance did. She wanted to curse her brother for it. Instead, she shrugged him off and gave a hard nod, daring him to call her a liar. She had to be up for this, if not for herself, then for those who depended on her. Ever since the attack she'd withdrawn from the world. Her absence left the orphanage and all the other places where she volunteered even more short staffed than usual. In some ways, that hurt worse than the impact on her personally. Her grip on the rifle tightened as she spun away and stalked toward the area Delilah had long ago set aside for paintball. "Better grab a gun from one of the boys," she called over her shoulder to her brother.

Silent and steady, the group fell in behind. She beat them to the clearing at the center of the combat zone by a good five minutes, earning her a frown from Jon. She pretended not to notice while she rechecked her weapon and adjusted her protective gear. She watched the others, purposely forcing herself to stare at the stupid red hats, denying the anxiety that built in her even as it caused her to tremble. Pissed off, she jammed an old, battered motorcycle helmet on her head, but didn't pull the visor down over her face.

"So, how's this going down?" Jon asked, once they were all geared up and ready.

At a loss, Suzanne looked toward Delilah, who stood across the way from her in old leathers, but no helmet. Lance's aunt stepped in without even a blink, giving Suzanne the time she needed to get her thoughts in line. "House rules: no crying foul when ya get hit, no magic, no firing across neutral territory, no head shots, no double-teaming no one. A hit takes you out of the round until you return to neutral ground and one of your team tags you back in." Delilah paused and nodded for Suzanne to continue.

"We're not out here for me to use you as target practice…" she said. "I have a problem I have to work through and I have to do it honest or there is no point. I need to get over this bullshit of freezing up every time I see…r-r…*Red*." Suzanne had to force the word out from between gritted teeth. She felt a rush of triumph as she said it, something she'd had trouble doing since the attack. "My job is to find and claim these three flags." Suzanne pulled the markers from her pocket and held them up. "My team…you help me with that and you protect my ass while I retrieve them. You guys…" she turned to those wearing the red caps, "have to try and reclaim your flags before I reach neutral ground…which is right here in the center…or until I nail your butts to a tree. An alert signal will go off when I've claimed a flag. We keep going until I capture all three, or you rescue them.

"And *no* going easy on me…" Suzanne caught each of their eyes. "Got it?"

They all nodded back.

That settled, Suzanne forced herself to look down at the flags, made an effort to actually see them, instead of staring past them. She took a deep breath, willing the crisp aroma of the autumn air to settle her, then drew upon her magic. It took just a touch of energy to lay her spell on them; a simple alert of sound and color to signal when she claimed each flag. Once done she held the markers out to Bubba's boys and one to Sammy as well. "You know what to do. You have ten minutes to plant your flags," she told them. "Then I want your butts back here and out of the war zone."

"All right!" the boys yelled and took off for the trees, each going in a different direction. Sammy went more sedately, if with no less haste. Of its own accord, Suzanne's gaze tracked Shawn, who whooped and brandished his flag in the air as if leading a charge. As the red flickered in and out of sight among the trees, a thin coat of sweat chilled Suzanne's exposed skin. Again her nerves crawled. Growling, she yanked her attention back to those waiting. They stood already grouped in their teams. She forced herself to go on as if she were fine, instead of ready to jump or lash out at every flicker of red. As soon as the boys returned, both teams faded into the forest.

The world closed in when Suzanne pulled her visor down into place, making sure it clicked securely. She focused on breathing, slow and deep, reminding herself she had plenty of air. She'd chosen an older model rifle, a Sheridan pump-action. Slower, but more reliable, it sat solid and comfortable in her grip. Suzanne charged it, dropping a ball into the chamber, and held it at the ready as she searched for the flutter of a flag.

Something flickered among the trees, barely seen out of the corner of her eye. Suzanne turned to face the direction full on but saw no flag, or anything else responsible for the movement. Scowling, she continued the turn, searching the zone, straining to pick up any sound. The only noise came from the boys, laughing as they fooled around in the clearing. *Cut it out,* she silently ordered herself, fed up with all her chicken-shit jumping at shadows.

The further she went, the more the sounds of laughter faded until only the leaves *shushed* overhead, occasionally overlaid by the trill of a brazen bird. Behind her another crow cawed, making her jump, and Suzanne had to resist the urge to turn it into a neon-painted corpse. It would take a lot of effort with an airgun, but that was the kind of mood she was in.

With her rifle at the ready, she wove her way through the trees, gaze sharp as she scanned the patch of woods. She spied movement ahead, to either side, about twenty yards off; she'd caught up to her teammates, who bisected the zone looking for the opponents' flags. Joining them in their efforts, she could almost swear she saw other activity as well, caught at the tail of her vision, off to the side...

The boys trying to sneak into the action? Or something else? Suzanne stopped with a jerk, bringing her weapon around, but found nothing there. The skin at the nape of her neck rippled as she turned a tight circle, trying to catch what always seemed just at the edge of sight. Was that a glimmer of brownish red? The gleam of pointed teeth? Flat, red-black eyes burning under the deadfall?

Sweat formed beneath her gear despite the cool temperature of the day. The more the others moved ahead, the more Suzanne noticed the forest scents on the air; predominantly moldering leaves, but beneath that, just the ghost of a smell, a faint coppery tang. She'd smelt it often…or thought she had, anyway…since she'd been rescued. Instinct had her wanting to curl in a ball around the acid bath churning her stomach. She resisted.

Then she realized what she did…creeping and skulking and feeding her phobia when she stood on *protected* land. Of course, it was easy to tell herself she was safe; it was all together harder to believe it when she couldn't shake the feeling of being watched. Still, imagined or not, Suzanne didn't—usually—hide from anything. It pissed her off. She hardly recognized herself. Spunk used to describe her quite aptly; now spooked seemed more applicable.

No, Suzanne thought to herself, fighting the urge to whimper. *Stop doing this to yourself or go home to Father, because you'll have proven him right!* The club wouldn't turn her away for having a problem, but she'd be letting them down nearly as much as herself if she didn't get a handle on this. It could even put them at risk. She'd walk away before letting that happen. But not just yet…she wasn't ready to cry "Uncle." Not even in her head.

Suzanne raised her visor and let loose a primeval battle cry, which her teammates echoed through the wold. Challenge cast, they all dashed off in divergent directions to find the flags. She barely noticed a tingle across her body, as if she'd just crossed the shield, even though the perimeter lay nowhere nearby. Caught up in the hunt, she dismissed the sensation.

An hour and a half later, Suzanne's team had claimed two flags. She had been back to neutral ground five times: twice to turn in the pennants and three times to get tagged back in to the game. She was tired and beat—by no means the same thing—and she was ready to wring the neck of the person responsible for placing the final flag. They'd clearly gotten... *creative.* She did have some idea who to thank. The last time she'd humped it back to the clearing, shaking ball fragments out of her shirt, Shawn had grinned so big his eyes disappeared, and it wasn't because she'd flashed any skin.

Let him grin, though, and let him gloat at his bit of mischief, whatever it was; Suzanne felt like grinning right back. Her plan worked better than she'd ever hoped it would. After hours of paintball, she barely felt a twinge now, not even when Gavin kept popping up out of nowhere to take pot shots at her. Some hesitation remained, but she didn't freeze up and curl into a ball the way she had just last night. Now if only she could find the blasted flag they could get back to *Delilah's!*

She didn't know the time—neither mages nor fae wore watches... something about their nature had a detrimental effect on the technology—but a glance at the position of the sun overhead placed it sometime after noon.

As she brought her gaze down from the sky, Suzanne swore the forest blue.

There, only yards away...and about twenty-five feet up the bole of an ancient sycamore...the third flag hung vibrant against the muted greens and browns and creams of the patchwork bark. Shawn, the little shit, had his father's sense of humor and apparently enough of his mother's pixie nature to make things interesting. Locking her jaw, Suzanne headed for the blaze of red canvas, scanning all around for any defenders lurking nearby. Seeing no one, she ran for the sycamore. She lacked the innate grace of the resident dryad, but thanks to her four-fold nature, in mere moments she'd scurried up the tree with the help of Earth and Wind. Only a slight tremor shook her hand as she set her jaw and snatched up the crimson flag. The canvas strip immediately went into her jacket pocket while the sky above her erupted in an indigo light display complete with muted fanfare.

"Game on," she called out, her voice throaty and full, charged with a fresh flood of adrenaline.

She moved by instinct and the force of momentum, barely aware of the answering challenge from below while she began her descent or the *thunk* of spattering paint that twice only just missed her at braced thigh and extended arm. She laughed again and aimed her charged weapon one-handed at red-capped Bubba. Barely flinching as she pulled the trigger, she allowed the recoil to send her spinning from her perch before the ball even impacted. Again taking advantage of her nature, she flowed down like a feather on the breeze and landed in a clear space between the trees, hitting the dirt in a controlled roll that brought her to her feet, already dashing full out for neutral ground.

"Damn, that stings!" Not for the first time, Bubba swore behind her as she disappeared into the forest, already yards away. She laughed, not at his pain, but with the joy of the game, at each little triumph over fear. From farther off she heard the sound of bodies rushing through the underbrush. More concerned with putting distance between her and the opposition than she was with being stealthy, Suzanne kept on running, bounding over fallen branches and dodging among the trees. If they tagged her now, she and her team would lose the game. Any moment she expected the solid *thunk* of a paintball to collide with her back.

Instead, the sounds of pursuit faded and the forest noises slowly increased: scurrying through the leaves, birdsong above, the blasted caw of the crows all around...she felt like the spell beacon still flashed over her head, drawing every eye in the forest to her. Of course, these days she always felt watched anyway, even when alone. Getting over her phobia of the color red hadn't banished that. Suzanne blocked it all out as she slowed to a walk, taking a moment to catch her breath and think. She couldn't run straight back or they'd be on her like anything, but if she went quiet and stealthy, and circled around to come in from another angle, she'd probably have a clear field.

Her steps moved both quick and sure through the undergrowth and deadfall. She set her jaw and straightened her shoulders. One yard...ten, a half-dozen more...She tensed with each step, but it didn't cripple her. Another success. A dangerous smile came across her lips.

Twenty feet ahead of her stood a clearing. At the center lay a small faerie ring, eight feet wide, maybe less; one of many that dotted the Wild Hunt lands. Altering her steps, she headed for the ring. Each one had a distinct feel. One she could recognize and identify. It would give her an idea of her location in the forest and which way she needed to go.

She stopped abruptly, taking a half a step back. In front of her, a wizened figure out of her most recent nightmares crept from behind the bole of a tree. *Redcap. Powrie. Dunter.* All names for the same vile fae, but she'd always think of them as redcaps. The image of them bathing those caps in her blood so haunted her no other name would serve.

Her stomach contracted painfully and her eyes locked onto the perverse leer on the redcap's face. His right hand curled around an iron pike, the left waggled its fingers at her, like an auld uncle relaxing by the fire. She took in his ironshod boots and the soft cap on his head, a bit more brown than red today. A distant memory niggled at her mind as she catalogued that fact, but the detail played hard to get. It had something to do with their nature... The knowledge remained elusive, which did not surprise her. She'd never paid much attention to the creatures, having nothing to do with redcaps before two weeks ago.

She wished she could still say as much.

How did he breach the shields? she couldn't help but wonder. Then the bastard licked his lips and looked her up and down, quite familiarly, distracting her from the thought.

Suzanne snarled. Here stood the first test of today's success. Combat instinct kicked in and she drew magic to her, the spell on her jacket clearing the way for her fins to unfurl, streaming violet tendrils of energy behind her. A growing metallic tang blanketed the aroma of wet leaves and decay she'd stirred up from the deadfall. It barely registered.

Suzanne faced one foe that she could see. He had not come alone. Somewhere in the forest she sensed more of the beastly fae lurking. Their voracious hunger clung to her like a fog on the air. It pulsed with each pounding beat of her heart until her skin twitched in protest against the sensation. The paintball field no longer filled her vision, obscured now by images from her personal hell. The awareness of being watched increased and the rising wind seemed to carry eager murmurs that had until this moment been relegated to Suzanne's nightmares. She recognized the sound before the feasting. The forest pulsed around her, at once the land behind *Delilah's*, yet reminiscent of the other forest where she'd first been attacked. The disorientation played havoc with her equilibrium.

"No!" she growled, rage conflicting with fear, drawing the outcry both long and loud. "Not this time. Buffet's closed."

The redcap laughed and took a step forward. Did Suzanne imagine the desperate edge to the sound? She couldn't say. Feeling a bit perverse herself, she aimed the Sheridan at him and fired. He moved before the ball tagged the trunk of the tree he'd been standing in front of, but then, that had been the point, hadn't it? As he dodged away, Suzanne raced for the clearing, readying her magic and charging the airgun while she closed the distance to her goal.

She heard scrabbling behind her; the sound of many feet converging, accompanied by grumbling and sick, slurping sounds. A gnarled hand grasped the bottom edge of her jacket with the strength of a bulldog. Her violent twist to the side broke his grip. She looked back and thought she saw several grinning faces at her heels, baring razor teeth and blood-red tongues. One followed close. Suzanne put on speed to out-distance him, but as her right foot came down across the mushroom ring, something yanked the other back. Suzanne pivoted and balanced on her free leg. She'd been caught by the one that had first stepped in front of her in the woods. She knew it was him because a few Pepto-pink splatters speckled his face. Hatred mingled with the hunger and murder in his expression. Not liking the look in his gleaming red gaze, she blasted him in the head again, this time with a screaming-orange paintball.

As he yipped and snarled at her, pushed back by the force of the gas-driven ball, she yanked her left foot out of his grip. Pain shot up her leg as she pulled free. Most of her, anyway; she'd lost more than skin in her effort to get loose. The redcap raised his hand and made a show of licking her blood and flesh from his clawed fingers. Though there wasn't much, the red of his hat still seemed to brighten. The memory niggled again. It lingered long enough for her to catch a piece of it. From within the faerie ring she used her magic to close it against them...and herself. Very important, that. Standing there, breath heaving, she slowly turned a circle as the redcaps converged. She found something unnatural in this, even for matters involving the Fae. Six of them surrounded her, all familiar, though she wished she could say otherwise. It was a rare thing for these solitary fae to band together.

She narrowed her gaze as her mind had no choice but to acknowledge that *her* blood dyed their caps. As long as they were wet with it, a bond existed between them. It let them spy upon her, it let them find her, and—she realized now—it let them pass the Wild Hunt's defenses, which had been keyed to let her through. That tingle! Damn, she had actually felt them cross the shield.

Something else still eluded her, but she found herself too distracted to pinpoint what. At the moment the creatures paced around her haven, stomping and grumbling and lashing out until their clawed hands set off sparks against the transparent barrier of her shield.

Agitated did not seem a strong enough a word for the actions of these murderous fae.

With a calm she did not feel and an urge to poke them further, Suzanne sat down to contemplate her situation—and the redcaps—more closely. Her left foot rested on the ground and she bent her knee, raising her pant leg and baring her bloody ankle. The redcaps grew frenzied. She had to laugh as they flung themselves at her, only to be sent flying back with a flash and a sizzle, repelled by her magic. Each time they rushed the shield, a shiver traveled through her at the impact, a disruption in the energy. The protection held, but for how much longer?

Then something occurred to her. She could leave. She didn't have to stay here. Didn't have to confront them. Didn't *need* to, did she? From within this gateway she could go anywhere in the Fae or mortal worlds with but a thought. Yet the question remained: if she fled would she ever be free of the hold they had on her? Her fingers tightened on the stock of her weapon as she considered that. The stink of her own sweat filled the magic-enclosed circle. Forcing herself to breathe deep, she realized something else. The terror tasted stale. Old. Done.

Yes, her pulse pounded, and yes, her muscles knotted, but the redcaps had not trapped or even overwhelmed her, merely had her outmanned. Sense had sent her scrambling, not fear. Adrenaline kept her tense and trembling, ready for action, not flight.

She found peace in the revelation.

Suzanne raised her left hand, tilted her head coyly to the side, and let her fingers waggle at the leader of the redcaps. Not even bothering to get up, she started the spell to open the gateway. Before she could complete it, a flicker of movement among the trees caught her eye, followed by a faint sound of roughhousing drawing nearer. She spied two familiar figures goofing off among the trees.

"Fuck!" she yelled aloud. She reacted out of pure instinct, not thought, scrambling to her feet with a twinge of pain from her ankle. The gate spell remained partially formed around her, giving the air a rippled effect. Combined with the effect, her sudden movement drew all eyes to her, those far away and those up close. The movement she'd noticed stopped dead, as did the frenzy taking place directly around her. Suzanne knew what she must do as the last bit of forgotten redcap lore surfaced. If the redcaps became aware of Bubba's boys, they'd be on them in an instant. They had no choice. If the caps upon their heads dried out, the creatures died. They might lust after her blood as a matter of pride—they were not known for leaving survivors—but any would do when it came down to their own survival. The unsuspecting boys represented the easier target. After all, the recaps could always target her again later, at their leisure, once their caps were properly moist and crimson.

Suzanne calmly slid her hand into her pocket and palmed the butterfly knife she'd stowed there. She brought it out and flicked it open in one smooth move, raising both arms over her head. She clenched her right hand into a fist then flicked her fingers wide, meaningless to the redcaps, but an order the boys knew well, to split up and scatter. Her effort came too late. Several of the redcaps turned away from her and began to stalk the boys. She couldn't allow that. Her other hand swept down, drawing the open blade in a shallow slice down the back of her right hand. As the blood welled, those redcaps that had broken off came rushing back again.

She had their attention now. For them, the world outside of her no longer existed. Tongues flicked and lips smacked as red-tinged eyes avidly followed the trail of blood snaking down her sleeve. Certain of their complete and focused attention, Suzanne willingly called upon Earth and Air and Fire and Water for the first time in her life, not quite knowing what she asked, but instinct telling her she must.

Nothing happened.

Well, nothing more than the wind lashing the forest into a thrashing maelstrom. The redcaps ignored it.

Suzanne's eyes closed and her head flung back, a flash of despair arching her spine. The brief moment of weakness broke her focus. Just enough. Down came the shield and Suzanne nearly dropped with it as the force of the winds hit her on the heels of the broken spell. The air around her shook and shattered as all six redcaps rushed the circle.

No. Not again. Never again, not for the feasting, not for the fear...with her or anyone else. Her eyes snapped open and her chin lowered until she met the redcaps' gazes with an unholy glare.

"Bring it," she growled, as she carefully, gently cut her spirit off from the connection to Lance, safeguarding him from what would come.

Her arms came down, ready and beckoning at her sides, and her knees bent, legs spreading a bit wider in a fighter's stance. At her back, her fins—flooding with magic—unfurled with a whip's crack, trailing tendrils of energy primarily colored in lavender and blue. She stood there in challenge while they rushed her. The winds continued to tug at her, one dry, one cool, one hot, and one wet. Other than to brace herself, Suzanne barely had a chance to wonder at them before the redcaps descended, clutching and tearing. The leader—looking more painter's cap than redcap—fairly scaled her, catching the seam at her shoulder with his dagger-like nails, slicing right through her leather jacket to flesh. He laughed evilly as he rubbed his head—and his cap—against the flow like a macabre cat. As the others tore with less success at her leathers, Suzanne could think of only one more option, one way to ensure the boys' safety, and her release from this hateful link. She brought the shields back up again, encapsulating herself, the redcaps, and the errant whirlwind. Her mind turned inward as she held two things alive in her thoughts: first a spell to bind the redcaps to her, no matter how they sought to flee, and the second a destination. Once all six gripped her, she loosed her magic and ordered the gate to whisk them away.

Suzanne barely noticed that the winds followed.

The seven of them landed on the hard, superheated floor of the paint-drying furnace Suzanne used to run. The wicked fae shrieked as their flesh seared away. Five of the redcaps would never rise again; they burned to cinders around Suzanne as their caps dried out in an instant. Her nose pinched against the acrid stench. The ashes whipping around the chamber, borne upon the unnatural wind, stung her eyes, but the extreme temperature did not harm her. The rogue winds wove around where she crouched, insulating her from the intense heat of the furnace.

The sixth redcap, the leader, clung to her leg, apparently within the scope of whatever protected her. Half of his cap remained fresh-soaked and his gaze promised retribution. Suzanne couldn't breathe, but she lashed out at him. With a sharp jab, she slammed her right fist into his face; with the left hand, she swiped the crimson hat off his head, blood dripping from her fingers as she crumpled it in her fist and shoved it into the pocket of her jeans.

The redcap fell away from her with a shriek. Hatred and malice burned bright in his eyes like embers as he reached for her too late. His skin crackled and flaked away in an instant, like paper flash-incinerated. The memory of his expression lingered even as his ashes fell away.

Suzanne gasped, fully expecting she foresaw the means of her own death.

Instead, the winds swirled tighter around her. Again she felt the separate currents, sensed what she'd missed before as Earth gently cradled her flesh, Air filled her lungs, Fire drew away the painful heat, and Water cooled her scorched throat. That safeguarding done, the Four Winds wrapped around her in a protective funnel and lifted her away, back through the newly opened gate.

She came to on the forest floor, in the middle of the neutral ground, blinking up into ten anxious faces. Her helmet and rifle lay on the ground beside her. A grin came to her face as she fumbled with her jacket pocket, pulling out a crumpled canvas flag. "I win," she crowed as she held it aloft, and only four of those staring down at her knew how thoroughly.